Monday
I Love You

By the Same Author

The Love Letters of J. Timothy Owen

Monday I Love You

Constance C. Greene

HARPER & ROW, PUBLISHERS
Cambridge, Philadelphia, San Francisco, St. Louis, London, Singapore, Sydney
New York

11.89

Library of Congress Cataloging-in-Publication Data
Greene, Constance C.
    Monday I love you / by Constance C. Greene.
        p.   cm.
    Summary: A teenage girl with a poor self-image gains
self-esteem with the help of a sympathetic teacher and
a childhood friend.
    ISBN 0-06-022183-6: $
    ISBN 0-06-022205-0 (lib. bdg.): $
    [1. Self-respect—Fiction.]   I. Title.
PZ7.G8287Mo–1988
[Fic]—dc19   87-27084
                                                  CIP
                                                  AC

8888133

For Judith with Love

Monday
I Love You

1

I am the most popular girl in the entire tenth grade. I am long and lean and sinuous. My hair is golden and fits my head like it was made for it. My eyes are bright Paul Newman blue and my eyelashes are fantastic. I am one of those people everyone wants to look like. People say I will go far, although in what direction no one dares hazard a guess. My mother and father are rich and powerful and smell good. Our house smells of flowers and Mr. Clean. We swim in our pool on hot nights and drink lazily from long, tall frosted glasses. We eat steak quite a lot. There isn't anything in this world I want that I don't or can't have. My sweaters are stacked neatly, according to color: stacks of red, gray, blue, yellow. You get the picture. My shoes are lined up with shoe trees inside them. Each shoe is polished to a gloss so high it'd put out your eye. My closet seethes with gorgeous garments.

My father wears fourteen-karat-gold cuff links in his French cuffs. And Gucci loafers. My father is tall and handsome, an honest investment banker with a salary in six figures. My father went to Harvard and sails his own sailboat to Bermuda anytime he wants. He also flies his own airplane and has never had an accident. My father always wanted a daughter.

My mother smiles and the world is hers. Her laugh is low and loving, and when she comes to see if I'm asleep, her hands are smooth and gentle. My mother pours tea from her heirloom silver teapot and we have plates of cucumber sandwiches all over. My mother has three fur coats and a diamond necklace, which she plans to leave me in her will. If she dies first, that is.

Lucky, you say. I can hear you saying Lucky. I wish I was her.

My life is that of a princess. Or a rock star.

Where do I go from here?

Good question.

The life above is lies. All lies. I lie a lot. Or call it making up stories. I learned how to do it from William. He was excellent at that. I sometimes think of William and wonder what happened to him—if he's still making up bigger and better stories at the drop of a hat.

If it makes me feel better, what's the harm? It's okay

if it makes you feel better, right? I have a tremendous capacity for deluding myself. This sustains me in my dark hours, which are many and very dark. It's okay. The only person who might be hurt by my lies is me. Myself. I.

You have to have something to strive for in this life. You have to have goals. Something that's an impossibility. Hard work will bring you friends and riches and respectability.

Lies. All lies.

I wear a 38D bra. I'm saving up to have an operation to reduce the size of my breasts. They make fun of me on account of my huge boobs. I know it. I hear them laughing. Boys brush by me in the hall. That's so they can claim they felt my breasts. Humongous, the word goes out. And all hers, they snigger. I know that. It doesn't bother me. All those flat-chested little girls envy me.

I read in a medical magazine that if you can get a doctor to say the health of his patient depends on her having her boobs made smaller, the insurance company will pay half the cost of the operation, which is plenty. I think it's safe to say my health, my mental health, definitely depends on my having this operation.

"Look at it this way, Grace," my friend Estelle says. "Lots of those turkeys would give their eyeteeth to have your bust." I wish Estelle wouldn't call it a bust. I've asked her not to, but she calls it a bust anyway.

"Throw back your shoulders, Grace," my mother says. "Stand tall. Carry yourself proudly. You have my mother's bust. Be proud of it."

If there's a God in heaven, why did he let me wind up with my grandmother's bust?

Estelle is plump, plumper even than I am. She has little brown eyes and a Tina Turner hairdo that her mother, who is a hairdresser, blows dry for Estelle every morning. Before she goes to school. Estelle has the chicest hair of any girl in school.

I sometimes wonder. What is it that makes Estelle and me friends? Is it because she's fatter than me? If Estelle were thin, would she be my friend? If I were thin, would I pick Estelle to be my best friend?

Grace is an old-fashioned, phewey name. I hate it. My mother's name is also Grace. So is my busty grandmother's. Big Grace, middle-sized Grace and teeny tiny Grace. Right.

It's a known fact that Americans are obsessed by thinness, by facial and bodily beauty. By success. If I have my breasts cut down, and overnight shed twenty-five pounds by cutting back on fats and fries, and smile a lot, maybe they won't notice my lack of facial beauty. You have to keep telling yourself you don't care. You know that inside you're a very nice person. A good person, who is kind and caring and giving. The kind who, when somebody's short a penny at the checkout counter, hands over a penny of their own money and says, Here, you don't have to pay it back. I've done that more times than I can count. Plenty of times. Once I handed over a dime to a little runty kid with a quart of milk and a runny nose. "Here," I said, when the check-out girl scowled and said, "You're short a dime, sonny. Cough up the right change or put it back."

"Here," I said again, and head down, hand out, the kid took my dime, flipped it at the girl and scuttled off. No thanks, no nothing to me, his benefactor. Even so, I felt good, knowing I'd helped. If it'd been Christmas Eve and snowing, I'd have felt even better. But it was August with the flies decorating the strips of flypaper like cloves stuck in a country ham. And even if that kid ran like a jackrabbit, the chances were the milk soured on him before he hit his front stoop.

Once my father called from Texas looking for funds. He was onto something big, he'd said. Two hundred ought to tide him over until the gusher gushed.

My mother just snorted at him away off there in Texas and said, "Trust you. The oil boom's over." When she wants, my mother can be a big downer. She has a mean mouth on her when it suits her.

"If anyone asks, Grace," she told me, "your father's an entrepreneur."

"How do you spell it?" I asked, and that was the end of that.

Most of all, I would like someone to talk to. Really talk, I mean, not just move lips so words come out.

Exchange thoughts and ideas. Estelle and I talk a lot, say things like "He can put his shoes under my bed anytime." Or discuss what Sandra in *Leftover Life to Burn* should do. Sandra is known to have snuffed fertility pills like there's no tomorrow. So now she's pregnant with quintuplets. Sandra couldn't wait to have a baby, but now that there are going to be five of them, she's not so sure.

Estelle and I don't ever talk about anything really deep, stuff that matters. Mostly we talk about boys, about which neither of us knows squat. There's a boy in our class named Walter. They call him Croc, short for crocodile. He *does* sort of look like one. Estelle makes fun of him, of his looks, his clothes. He's the kind of person people make fun of. He's sort of spaced out, sort of out of things; he's quiet, and if he's in a group or something, he doesn't say a word. He hardly talks at all. Sometimes it's as if he doesn't exist; nobody eats lunch with him or walks down the hall with him. Even people who make fun of Croc don't get too much satisfaction from it, I guess, because he doesn't rise to the bait. Mostly he just slopes in and out of class, trying to make himself invisible. Once I caught him looking at me. I smiled, and he got up and walked out of the cafeteria. That got me flustered. I guess I don't know how to deal with being looked at. I told myself I should make friends with Croc. Everyone should have *one* friend, it seems to me.

I'd like someone to bare my soul to. Someone to love, someone who would cherish me. I've never been cherished. Someone who could say anything to me and to whom I could say anything back, and whatever I said would be understood and respected.

That's a lot to ask for.

2

My mother sells cosmetics door-to-door. She carries them in a stretched-out-looking suitcase studded with patches of mold. Our house is damp. Sometimes I lie in bed, and if I slit my eyes just right, the mold looks like flowers inching their way toward the ceiling. Delicate, fragrant flowers any person would be proud to have in their room.

"Here now." My mother is fond of demonstrating her selling technique. Reaching out with one shiny red fingernail, she places a deft stroke of blusher where it'll do the most good. Once a customer invited my mother to her wedding, her third. "If it wasn't for you," the customer said, "I'd have never landed the guy." After my mother went out and bought a new dress, the guy bolted. Took off in the middle of the night in a souped-up Grand Prix with a bum muffler. So much for a spot of blusher where it'll do the most good. My mother carefully folded her new dress, price tag dangling conspicuously.

"One thing life's taught me, Grace," she said sourly. "Never remove the price tag until after the main event."

Right now the cosmetics business is in a slump, so she's helping out in Estelle's mother's salon, doing manicures and facials. The salon happens to be in Estelle's mother's kitchen, which explains why the ladies often exit with their bouffants smelling of pork chops. Estelle's mother's tried everything, every deodorant spray going, but nothing works. I suggested maybe it'd be good if they moved the salon to their basement playroom, but Estelle said her father would blow his cork. He's got his gun collection down there and a bar with flashing lights and a spigot that shoots out beer he made himself. He's not about to turn his game room into a hairdressing place, Estelle says, in one of her edgy moods.

My mother also waxes people. Gets rid of unwanted hair—on lips, armpits, thighs, stomachs even. She says you wouldn't believe the places people have unwanted hair. Once she put hot wax on a woman's mustache, and when she pulled off the cooled wax, a strip of skin came with it. The customer threatened to sue. My mother calmed her by promising her a free wax job. My father, relaxing in his recliner, said, "How about a free lube job too?" and my mother, eyes glittering, poured his newly opened can of beer down the kitchen sink, oblivious to his cries of "Hey, I was only kidding!"

"Anyone can make a mistake," my mother said. "Look at who I married."

When my mother and father fell in love, she was quite plump, my mother told me. "Not fat, you understand," and she eyed me, making me blush and fold my arms across my chest.

"Pleasingly plump," she continued, frowning at me. "Grace, you must learn not to be ashamed of your form." Form. What a dumb word for big boobs. "Hold yourself like a queen, like you're wearing a diamond tiara," she told me. "Be proud of your God-given body."

"Hey, fat mama." A thin, ferret-faced boy whistled in my ear last week. "Hey, there, fat mama. Let's us have some fun, fat mama."

I went to the girls' room and cried.

I started to develop when I was ten. I was the only girl in the fifth grade who had a shape. Right away I knew it was a mistake. I began going around with my shoulders hunched, arms crossed, trying to conceal myself. The piles of books I carried to school grew bigger and bigger until they were so heavy I started getting pains in my chest. My mother took me to the doctor, thinking something was wrong with me. Well, actually, there *was* something wrong, but not what she thought. Not a thing easily cured.

The doctor was a kind woman, about a size nine, I'd

guess. She suggested my mother buy me some sweaters larger than the one I was wearing, and, "Be patient, things will get better," she said. Adding I would grow into myself.

After the doctor we went for a soda. "Well, I must say." My mother chased her maraschino cherry around and around until she caught it, scooped it out and laid it on the saucer. "I must say my little girl's not so little anymore. What will they think, a great big girl like you with a dainty little person like myself for a mother? What will people think?" and she smiled and patted my hand.

"My little Grace is on her way to womanhood." Ice cream gone, my mother sucked on her cherry, hanging on to it, not swallowing until she'd got all the good red juiciness out of it. No other mother talks the way mine does. I know because I listen to the way other mothers talk. Womanhood. My mother reads confession magazines and watches *Dynasty* and *Dallas* and all the soaps. No matter how raunchy they are, they don't seem to bring her up-to-date, and she gives it the womanhood bit. She's an anachronism, my mother.

"So." My father patted my shoulder when we got home. "So my girl's growing up." She didn't have to tell him about the visit to the doctor. She should've kept it between the two of us. At ten, I was catching up fast with my father. Soon I'd be taller than he was. That should give you some idea of the condition of my life.

Last month while my father was on his most recent search for fame and fortune, my mother called the Goodwill and they came and toted off his recliner. When my father returned, empty-handed, he started to lie down in the place the recliner had always reclined and almost fell on his butt.

Small as he is, it's amazing how my father swells up when provoked. It's like he swallows some mysterious potion that makes him three times his usual size.

"Where is it?" he bellowed, wild eyes raking the room. "What did you do with it, woman?"

My mother ran her tongue around inside her mouth rapidly, and her face got slick and shiny, the way it does when she's warming up.

"Goodwill got it," she stated. "It was old, anyway. A mess. You said you weren't coming back. What do you expect? I never know where I am with you," she complained, perching on the edge of the couch, ready for lift-off. "It's more than most people could stand, this on-and-off stuff. Off and on, there you go. My friends say I'm a fool to put up with it. With you. My mother was right. She said never marry a man with small feet. If they have small feet, she said, it's ten to one they have a high opinion of themselves. That's your problem, a high opinion of yourself." Then my mother's face crumpled and she blew loudly into the tissue she keeps stuffed up her sleeve ready for just such emergencies.

My father, looking stunned but proud, put his arm

14

around her tentatively. She nestled her hairdo into his thin shoulder and they sat on the couch together, speechless with emotion. I left the room, feeling in the way. My mother and father enjoy a roller-coaster relationship—up, down, down, up. Never on an even keel. Just when I think it's all over, they start snuggling. At least they have each other. I don't have anyone. And probably never will.

I went to my room and lay down without turning on the light. The radio was playing a bunch of golden oldies—Benny Goodman, Artie Shaw, Glenn Miller. Music to dance to. One thing I never tell anyone—this type of music soothes me, stirs my insides. I guess I'm an anachronism too. I've never been to a dance. I don't know how to dance. But I've seen them slow dancing, bare arms wrapped around the boy's neck, his arms locked around her, holding her. I've seen them. I know how they look.

The band played "Deep Purple," one of my all-time favorite golden oldies. "Deep Purple" makes me feel all shivery and warm. I absolutely love it. When it ended, I switched stations and wound up with a song about damaged relationships. All those damaged-relationship songs make me sick. I've never had *any* kind of relationship, damaged or otherwise, but I think there have to be a few relationships that are good. I guess those kinds aren't worth writing songs about though.

As I was getting drowsy, some guy with a raspy voice

15

sang about surfing, the high he got from riding a big one, with a raucous rock guitar making wave noises in the background. It was so real I almost got seasick.

Long after I heard my mother and father go to bed, heard their door close, heard the hum of their voices, then quiet, I lay with my eyes closed, unable to sleep.

At fifteen, I decided, nobody takes you seriously except yourself.

3

I was eight when I finally figured out I was a kidnapped kid. Watching a TV special after school, it came to me in a flash: My mother and father had snatched me from my carriage when I was an infant. That's why I looked so different, so unlike either of them. I felt a great rush of relief at finally knowing, a sense of triumph at having figured it out for myself.

Be on the lookout, the TV special warned. Constant vigilance is the only answer. Never leave your child alone, not for a second. The world is full of sickos, weirdos, wackos, on the prowl for children left un-tended. No one is safe. The program told about infants being taken from their mothers' arms in maternity wards, children disappearing from right in front of their houses, children disappearing from park benches, sandboxes or tricycles when the mother's head is turned for only an instant. Children never seen or heard from again. Children snatched by a slitty-eyed stranger driving a foreign car who offers them candy. Tell your children to never talk to strangers, never accept food or candy or a ride from strangers. The candy might be spiked with dope, and when the kid eats it, he falls in a faint and the weirdo shovels the kid into the car and zooms off. Never take your eye off your kid because the world is full of nuts.

Well, you'd think such a program would strike fear into a child's heart. Not into mine it didn't.

"So that's it!" I hollered, although there was no one home to hear. I snapped my fingers loudly in the silence. Then I got a glass of juice and a cracker and sat on the floor to play solitaire. I always played solitaire when I got home from school. I always won, too, though sometimes I had to cheat. What did it matter? I only cheated myself. Sometimes I asked a kid to come home with me and play. Mostly they said no. They never asked me to their houses. Except once. It was a new girl named Monica who asked me to her house, but she never asked me back. I didn't mind a whole lot. Even at eight I was getting used to being alone.

When my mother got home, dragging her suitcase with all her cosmetics inside, I said, "It's okay. I know all about it. You don't have to explain," and went right on shuffling the cards.

"What are you talking about, Grace?" she asked ir-

18

ritably. "If there's something bothering you, get it off your chest." Back then, it *was* a chest.

"I know I'm kidnapped," I said smugly, not displeased by the idea. At eight, I fancied myself telling all my classmates I was a kidnapped child. It might make a difference, I thought, might make me popular. Different, but in a good way. Then when they knew I was a kidnapped kid, they'd ask me over.

"I know where I came from," I said, slapping down the ace of diamonds.

"Have you been talking to someone about the Facts of Life?" my mother snapped. Even then I knew that nothing bugged her like sex lectures. She figured fifteen, sixteen, was early enough for that.

"No," I said. "I mean where I *really* came from." I smiled slyly at her. "You snatched me out of my carriage and brought me home. It's okay, though. I don't mind." The more I thought about it, the more romantic and touching I found the whole idea. My natural parents were out there somewhere, searching for me, their stolen baby girl. The next time I went downtown, I thought, I'd keep an eye out for them. I'd recognize them immediately, I felt sure.

My father, tall and handsome as ever, would be standing there with his gold cuff links winking in the sun. Anyone with eyes could tell he'd gone to Harvard and had a six-figure salary and a sailboat and flew his own plane. There are certain things that are hard to hide. And my mother would smooth my forehead with her gentle hands, and her sable coat would tickle my cheek as she hugged me to her.

"We've found you at last," my father and mother would exclaim as one. "I never gave up hope," my father would say, tears filling his eyes. "Neither did I," my mother would say, dabbing at her eyes with her pure-linen handkerchief.

Then they'd bring me home to my false parents, who, fearing I was dead, would hug and kiss me, weeping grateful·tears for my safe return. I felt very loved suddenly. So that's the way it goes, I thought. All four of them want me.

My mother felt my forehead, testing me for fever.

"Grace, what's the matter? Are you all right? What's this nonsense you're talking? Of course you're not a kidnapped child! How could you think such a thing! You were born right here in Spring Valley. Right over at the Spring Valley hospital, on the fourth floor. Willis delivered you. Of course he's dead now, but he did deliver you. It was such a lovely day, too. Blue sky and a little breeze. I won't hear any more nonsense. Not after the day I've had. Oh, my poor feet." My mother laid the back of her wrist against her forehead and closed her eyes.

I·studied her face a long time. She *was* telling the truth. I could always tell. I was crushed. My moment in the sun, the light of so many people's lives, had been brief.

"Then if you're my real mother," I shouted at her,

not caring about her poor feet, "how come I don't have a brother or sister to play with? If you're my real mother, you would've had someone for me to play with. I want somebody to play with!" I stamped my foot, having a first-class temper tantrum, something I'd wanted to do for a long time. Usually I was a placid child, eating what was put in front of me and never giving any trouble. Now, I felt the blood running high in my veins, could feel my heart thumping and thudding around inside me. I was surprised, looking down at myself, not to see my skin being pushed in and out by my thumping heart.

At last, my mother opened her eyes and stared at me for a long minute. "Calm yourself, Grace," she said softly. "I've brought us some chop suey for supper. Just what you like—chicken, with noodles. And fortune cookies. Look in the bag." I opened the brown paper bag she'd brought home, reached in and took out a fortune cookie. When I bit into it, my fortune fell into my lap.

" 'Today,' " I read aloud, " 'you will make a new friend.' "

4

"Well, hi there, Grace. How's it going?"

I was washing my hands in the girls' room, leaning over the basin, letting the warm water run. I had nothing else to do. I found the feel of the water comforting. I squinted up, looking to see who had spoken. The voice wasn't familiar.

It was Ashley. Ashley of the beautiful bones, president of lots of things. Auburn haired, long legged, green eyed, sleek, small bust—in her case, a legitimate bust—small hips. Cashmere sweaters. Ashley had never spoken to me before. Directly, that is. Once or twice, when we passed in the lunchroom or the hall, I had been aware of her, for how was it possible not to be aware of Ashley,

22

and out of the corner of my eye saw her whispering to her friends, who slid their eyes over at me and laughed uproariously.

I ducked my head, wondering why she was speaking to me now, not wanting to meet the full force of her glacial green stare without some preparation. Why? Did she want to know me better? Had she heard rumors that behind this outrageous facade, I was a scintillating, fascinating person? That the truth was, regardless of my appearance, she wanted to ask me to her next slumber party? Or Sunday brunch? I had heard of Ashley's Sunday brunches, and the mere thought of attending one sent sharp stabs of anxiety and longing thrashing around in my insides. What did one wear to a brunch, Sunday or not?

Perhaps we'd sit on Ashley's porch exchanging stories, jokes, anecdotes, full of goodwill and carrot cake. Only the most popular girls, the sexiest, most athletic boys, went to Ashley's, were her friends. Ashley was It.

"I was noticing your sweater," Ashley purred. "Did you make it yourself?" Her long fingers grazed my shoulder. "It's gorgeous."

I almost said I didn't know you knew my name. My sweater was from K Mart's winter sale. All sales final. It was fake angora—sort of pale green and pink, with padded shoulders that made me look like a linebacker. I'd bought it for myself, thinking it might make me look less bulky. Instead, it did the reverse. But I was stuck with it. I stared down at her hand upon me, gathering courage to look directly at her. When I did, I saw a girl named Chloe.

Where did their mothers find these names? I wondered.

Chloe was standing slightly behind Ashley, as a good handmaiden should. I've read about handmaidens in history. Handmaidens are subservient creatures, ready to do the bidding of the lady of the manor or the queen.

"Hello," I said. To both of them. And went on washing my hands, uncertain of what was expected of me.

"Don't you think Grace's sweater is super?" Ashley's voice rose. I think she was trying to keep from laughing out loud. Chloe's eyes never left me. She didn't smile. I wondered why Ashley had chosen Chloe as her handmaiden when Chloe wasn't even that good-looking.

Behind me, someone stood in the girls'-room door, foot wedged in the crack to hold it closed. I turned off the water and reached out for some paper toweling. Chloe took my arms in an almost friendly way. Ashley reached out and began to unbutton my sweater.

I hunched my shoulders, hands still wet, and turned to escape. The smell of danger was everywhere.

Ashley ran her hand lovingly down my front, over my breasts, patting them with little love taps.

"Oh, Grace," Ashley pleaded, "just let us see you. All we want is to see if you're for real." Her fingers continued to unbutton me, and the one with the foot in the door took my other arm. Her name was Nicole. She was captain of the basketball team.

Luckily I had my blouse with the back zipper on under my sweater.

"Oh shit," Ashley swore under her breath. "Take off your blouse, dear Grace. Please." She actually smiled as she eased my sweater off and let it lie in a vast puddle on the cold tile floor. "We only want to see you. We promise not to tell anybody. If you promise not to tell anybody too. It's like a pact, Grace. It's between us girls."

A leaky tap was the only sound. I thought I heard music. The band was practicing in the gym, probably.

"Let go of me." My voice sounded so weak, so terrified, I knew it wouldn't stop them. Nothing was going to stop them. They held both my arms tightly as Ashley fumbled at the neck of my blouse. In one deft movement, she ripped it straight down to my waist. A long, hissing sigh, like escaping steam, drowned out the sound of dripping water.

I had on two bras. The one on the bottom was too small, and pale gray from long use. I thought two would make me look smaller. The one on top was my best one. It was black. Lace.

"Well, for God's sake, she's all dressed up," I heard someone, maybe Chloe, say.

"Yeah, and no place to go."

"Don't that beat all."

I felt fingers at my back, trying to undo my bra. Bras. "No," I said. "You're not. I won't let you."

"Cheese it." Nicole tore herself away to peer out the door. "The cops." They dropped me and left. Afterward, I remembered how Ashley sauntered, taking her time. Cool. Oh, so cool.

"Ho, Ms. Govoni," I heard her say.

Nothing to be done about the blouse. I was crying so hard I couldn't see. I had my sweater almost on when Ms. Govoni, the gym teacher, came in.

"Oh, you startled me," she said. "Just checking. Thought I smelled smoke." Arms flailing, panic-stricken, I mumbled something.

"Here, let me help." I felt Ms. Govoni touch me and I screamed, unable to control myself.

"Let me alone!" I shouted.

"Grace. I'm terribly sorry." She sounded a long way off. "I was only trying to help."

I fled into one of the stalls, locked myself in and began flushing the toilet, trying to drown out the awful sounds I couldn't stop making. A piece of my blouse hung down outside my sweater. In a rage, I tore it off and scuffed it into a corner.

I couldn't stop crying. The sobs came from my feet. They shook me, preparing the way for more. All of my life I would remember their faces, the feel of their hands. All of my life, I knew they would go on destroying me with their indecency. If I could have killed them at that instant, I would have, gladly.

"Please, Grace." Between seizures, I heard Ms. Govoni tapping on the stall door. "Let me help. Please."

I didn't answer. When you're not used to kindness, it's tough to handle. Eventually, I stopped. I don't know how long I stayed in there. At last, when I unlocked the door and came out, Ms. Govoni was waiting.

She handed me a fistful of tissues. I took them and blew. I didn't look at myself in the mirror. I knew that crying, even a small fit of crying, made me look like a piece of Spam—mottled, red, meaty looking. I turned on the cold water and stuck my head under.

"I'm not asking what happened," Ms. Govoni said after a while. "I know you won't tell me anyway. Not now." She checked her watch. "I'm through for the morning. Would you like to come out with me and have some coffee?"

I didn't want coffee, but I didn't want to be alone. I couldn't go back to class, looking the way I looked. There was no point in going home. So I said, "Yes, I'd like some coffee."

"I'll notify your homeroom teacher," Ms. Govoni said. Her whistle hung outside her sweatshirt. Kids made fun of Ms. Govoni. Her hair was messy, bunched over her ears. They said she looked like a spaniel and liked girls better than boys.

"Mine's the red Subaru wagon, license plate GYM–3," she said. "Vanity plates." She smiled at me, and without knowing if I still knew how, I smiled back. "Here are the keys. Wait for me. I won't be a minute."

I ran through the halls and out into the parking lot, unlocked the car and got in. I stared hard at my lap, thinking it had got a lot fatter since the last time I'd looked at it, wondering how and if I'd be able to go on with my life as if this hadn't happened. Wondering if I'd tell on them, knowing I wouldn't.

I'm telling. Like a six-year-old, I'm telling.

Maybe we could move, go someplace else. Maybe my father'd get a job somewhere else. Lord knows we'd moved plenty in the past. Why couldn't we move one more time?

What would that solve? You take yourself with you, some wise man once said. I was my own baggage, large and cumbersome baggage.

I emptied my head of everything. I'd taught myself to do that when bad things happened. Things I couldn't face, couldn't cope with. I simply thought of nothing.

5

"Which one is you?" Estelle had asked when I showed her the glossy photo of the Gathering of the Schmitt Clan my mother had framed and hung over the living-room sofa. When I pointed to a dark and scowling child third from the left in the front row, Estelle said, "I'd know you anywhere."

Why'd you ask then? I wondered.

Nobody warns you about turning five. It seemed I'd started out all right, then when I hit five I turned fat and ugly. They're always full of stuff about watch out for puberty, the teen years are the worst, all that. Nobody says a peep about five. Baby pictures have me smiling, cute as a button, even if my legs are a little stubby and my clothes pull against my waist. Then I went to kindergarten. A whole new world lay out there, one I wasn't sure I could handle.

My mother held my hand. I remember that much. Her other hand held her cosmetics suitcase. The room blared with light; little tables and chairs stood waiting. The room was full of kids in various stages of anxiety. Some of them looked smug. They were the ones who knew how to write their names and even read a little. But their faces wore smug looks just as surely as their feet wore new shoes. The smell of new shoes was very strong in the room. I always associate the smell of new shoes with kindergarten. There was a blackboard and piles of clean erasers. Lots of chalk. We were instructed to sit at one of the little tables and fold our hands and wait for further orders. Wait until the teacher got her act together.

The teacher didn't look a whole lot bigger than the children, I remember. I've thought about that some since and decided they pick kindergarten teachers for their small stature rather than for their ability to lead children through the paths of higher learning.

When they took the roll call and the teacher called out, "Grace? Grace Schmitt?" in an unnecessarily loud voice, I panicked. The name sounded familiar to me but not enough to make me raise my hand. Saying "Here" was out of the question. I remember it seemed like a long morning. Midmorning we had juice and crackers, and the rest was downhill all the way.

I longed for the comfort and security of my own

30

backyard and a bathroom with only one toilet. All those toilets confused me. And, instead of doors, they had little droopy red curtains to shield us from curious eyes. I went into each stall, praying for a door, but all I got was another droopy red curtain. Kids ran in and out, poking their fingers at me, issuing shrieks as they ran that made me think of wild birds. It was very unsettling.

Just as I was getting to like kindergarten, getting used to it and all the strange children and the red curtains, our teacher told us we'd be moving on.

"Just think, children," she said, clapping her little hands with glee, "in the fall you'll all be first graders. You'll be in school *all day*! Won't that be grand?"

I was dismayed. I wanted to stay put. I was the kind of child who didn't adjust easily, who preferred the familiar to the strange.

"Can't I just stay here? With you?" I whispered. But no one heard me.

Then another, even stranger event occurred: a family reunion.

I'd never been to a family reunion until an invitation came for the Gathering of the Schmitt Clan. My mother made me a new dress for the occasion. It was pink and ruffly and so short my underpants hung out. It did nothing for me.

When we got there, a skinny girl named Cora came up to me and pushed her face into mine. "I'm seven," said Cora, "and I'm gifted and talented." I cringed, being neither. "I thought they were going to give you back," she said in a snippy way. "My mother told me when your mother and father knew you were on the way, they said they'd give you back if you weren't a boy. But I see they didn't." Then she stuck her tongue out at me and put one finger in the middle of my stomach, just about belly-button level, and stepped on my feet.

Then the kissing began. I was stunned by what Cora had said, but even if I hadn't been, I would've hated all that spit. I felt as if I had spit all over my face. In my ears. Those were the spittiest kisses I can remember. Everybody kissed everybody else because they were related. My aunt Rena, my father's sister, came up to me and said, "Well, well," as if she didn't like what she saw, and planted a big juicy kiss on me. I backed off fast and landed on my uncle Ted's tassel loafers. Uncle Ted was a truck driver who liked to get out of his work clothes when he went anywhere. He spoke long and knowledgeably about semis and eight-wheelers, and he listed the good diners against the bad. Then Uncle Ted rolled up his sleeves to show me his tattoos. When he'd done with that, he pulled his shirt out of his belt to show off the tattoos on his stomach, and his wife came skimming across the ground, shouting, "Enough! Enough! This is a family gathering!"

As if I could forget.

There was a big, long table filled with food. The Schmitts were famous for their appetites. Our contribution was my mother's famous three bean salad. Her secret was letting it marinate for five days to get the most out of the beans. My father and I circled the table, avoiding my mother's three bean salad. There were so many cold cuts it might've been a deli, and endless bowls of cole slaw and potato salad.

Still they went on kissing. When the feast was over, I went out to the parking lot, found our car and huddled on the backseat to wait. I'll never forget how angry my mother was when at last she figured out where I was.

"Never do that again! Do you hear me?" she said over and over, taking me by the shoulders and shaking me, keeping time to what she was saying. "We thought you'd been abducted. Maybe been run over. We almost called the police. Never, never again do you do that, just disappear like that!" My father stood behind her, silent as the grave, smelling strongly of beer, nodding in agreement to everything she said. How was I to know "abducted" and "kidnapped" meant the same thing? If she'd said kidnapped right off, I never would've worked up that fantasy about being a kidnapped child.

My mother drove home, crouched low over the wheel as if ours was a getaway car and I held the swag. Now and then she'd make little *tsk tsk* noises with her tongue, thinking about what one of the relatives had said. Or worn. Or contributed to the food. Or about my hiding in the backseat. She didn't have much good to say about anybody or anything. But then, these were my father's relatives, Schmitts through and through. Not Parkers.

Parkers knew better. Parkers were higher class, she let us know. They would never do anything so common as to hold a family reunion.

Throughout her harangue, my father dozed. Or pretended to.

"I'm not going if they do," I said from the backseat. "I don't care what happens, I'm not kissing all those strangers ever again. Why should I let people kiss me just because they're my relatives? I'm not doing it," and I closed my eyes.

To my surprise, my mother cackled delightedly. I heard her even as I drifted off. She didn't often laugh, at me or anyone else. Or *with* me, either. Now, I think, she was doing both. I had won her favor without even trying.

We went over a pothole and the car lurched, waking me. "How come you decided to keep me?" I demanded.

"What? What? What's that you say, Grace?" My mother pretended she didn't know what I meant.

"Cora said you said you were going to give me back if I wasn't a boy," I said. "How come you changed your mind? Who were you going to give me back *to*? I bet nobody wanted me. Is that it? Nobody wanted me, so you had to keep me after all."

But my mother said nothing, only put her foot down hard on the gas pedal, and we sailed through the summer dusk, smashing bugs on our windshield left and right, as if she hadn't washed it just before we left home.

6

"What'll you have, girls?" The waitress poked her pencil daintily into the depths of her newly hennaed hair and waited.

"Coffee, all right, Grace?" Ms. Govoni said.

I nodded, thinking if I opened my mouth, I might get sick right then and there, making everything worse.

When the coffee came, it tasted bitter, as if it had been boiled. I drank it anyway.

"Sometimes it helps to put things into words." Ms. Govoni's voice was kind. "I know it's helped me on occasion."

I knew if I didn't tell someone, it would never go away. I would run the scene in the girls' room back and forth a hundred times, in slow motion, until it poisoned me. It would continue to eat into me and drive me crazy. I had to get rid of the pain and humiliation.

If I told my parents, they might think I'd made it all up.

"Okay. This is the way it was," I said, deciding.

I twisted my hands and cleared my throat. Ms. Govoni listened.

"This is it," I began again. Not sure I could go on. Maybe if she'd coaxed me, if she'd said anything at all, I might have decided not to tell. But she only sat quietly, waiting.

"Ashley." It was hard, saying her name. I swallowed and tried again. "Ashley said she wanted to see if I was for real. Here, I mean," and I touched myself. "She started to rip off my clothes so they could all see me naked. See if I was for real. They held my arms while she ripped. Then you came. If you hadn't, I don't know what would've happened. But you did."

I heard her draw in her breath sharply.

"Oh, Grace" was all she said. "Oh, Grace."

I didn't look at her. I didn't dare. I knew if I saw tears of sympathy in her eyes, it would start me off again. I'd cried enough. Tears get you nowhere. They only make you swell up, and make your face feel stiff and your eyes like slits in your face. Tears make you even uglier than before.

I'd made up my mind I wasn't going to cry anymore.

I waited while Ms. Govoni paid the check, uncertain

36

as to what I was going to do next. I wasn't going back to school, and that was that. Even if she tried to talk me into it, I wasn't going. I couldn't. Wild horses couldn't drag me.

But I should've known Ms. Govoni wouldn't try to make me.

"If you want, Grace," she said as we went out to her car, "I'll run you home. And when I get back to school, I'll make up some story—tell your homeroom teacher you weren't feeling well. Something. I won't tell what really happened. Unless you want me to." Her dark eyes were so kind, so full of compassion, I could hardly bear it.

"No," I said. "Don't tell them. I have to think about things. I don't want to go home, though. I think I'll just walk around. Thanks a lot. For everything. You've been very nice. I don't know what I'd have done without you. Thank you."

We shook hands.

"If I can be of any more help, Grace, I hope you'll call on me," Ms. Govoni said.

"Thank you." I was beginning to sound like a broken record. I watched her drive off, toward school, and began to walk. Putting one foot in front of the other took my mind off myself.

"I heard you went for coffee with Govoni," Estelle said accusingly next day after lunch break. "You look terrible. What happened?"

I rooted around inside my locker, pretending to look for something.

"Did something happen yesterday? They said something happened in the girls' room. Ashley was there, I heard. Bet she did something nasty. Or said something. I hate her. You can tell me, Grace. My lips are sealed."

I laughed. Half in, half out of my locker, I laughed so hard I thought I might be getting hysterical. Maybe I'd get stuck and they'd have to call the janitor to get me out. That'd be the icing on the cake. Me, stuck inside my locker, in hysterics.

All I could think of was an old World War II poster I'd seen that said LOOSE LIPS SINK SHIPS. I figured Estelle had the loosest lips in the county. Maybe the whole state.

"What's so funny? Meet me in the parking lot after last class." Estelle dangled her car keys enticingly. "Give you a ride home." Estelle had failed her driving test three times. The parallel parking loused her up. On the fourth try, she passed. I privately think they passed her to get rid of her. Now she gets to drive her mother's car to school if she does the shopping on the way home.

I would rather have walked, but it was starting to rain and I couldn't face the faces on the school bus. Word would've got around by now. They'd look at me, curious, wondering what went on, and I couldn't handle them. Not now.

Estelle is a terrible driver. She takes the back roads to avoid traffic. She says they're all out to get her. Even

38

on back roads she drives smack in the middle of the road, eyes peeled for deer, hubcaps and abandoned plastic garbage bags bulging with orange peels and worse. The one thing Estelle doesn't really expect to run across is another car. When one sometimes does come around a curve, catching Estelle with her pants down, so to speak, it's instant drama. The oncoming drivers' faces clench tight as any fist as they struggle to avoid a collision. Horns blaring, tires squealing, they hurl obscenities at Estelle, who drives on blithely. She can handle anything but an oncoming car.

When I got to the parking lot, it was raining hard.

"Get in," Estelle ordered, swinging open the door. "You look awful."

"You said that once," I told her. "If you're going to bug me, I'll walk."

We zoomed out of the parking lot, almost sideswiping another car, a '57 Chevy with fins a mile long and a red stripe painted around it.

"Ooooh, what I wouldn't give for a car like that!" Estelle said.

We headed for the A&P, Estelle shooting glances at me as she drove.

"Quit looking at me," I said. "Keep your eyes on the road."

"I heard you were crying in the girls' room," Estelle said again. We were stopped at the light at Park Street. "I heard you were having a fit. Is that true?"

I didn't answer.

"Okay for you." Estelle stared at me. The light changed and the car in back gave a little beep, telling us to move on. Estelle glared into her rear-view mirror. "Some people," she said, putting the car into third instead of first, bucking forward like the Lone Ranger's horse. Estelle's mother said if Estelle wanted to use her car, she'd have to learn to shift. She wasn't having her kid have it too easy, just put it in D and go. Driving shouldn't be made too easy, Estelle's mother said. Little did she know.

"What do I care? Do it your way. All I want is the straight story. I am your best friend, aren't I?" Still I didn't answer. Estelle spied a neighbor walking across the street. She waved madly, calling attention to herself.

"Keep your hands on the wheel," I said in a cold voice.

"Hey, whose car is it anyway?" Estelle snapped.

"Your mother's," I reminded her. "And believe me, if she saw the way you horse around when you're driving her car, she'd blow a gasket."

"Who's to tell her?" Estelle's eyes got smaller as her cheeks came up to meet them.

I shrugged. "Oh, maybe that person you waved to might. Anybody. One of her customers. 'Oh, Helen, I saw your daughter downtown today,'" I imitated the customer. " 'She was carrying on something fierce, causing a traffic tie-up. Driving your car. I couldn't believe my eyes. Aren't you a brave thing, turning your car over to her.' "

"Oh shut up," Estelle said. I sat in the car while she went in to buy fat-free milk, strawberry yogurt, a bag of Fritos and a six-pack of diet soda. They snack a lot in her house.

On the way home I suggested we stay on the main road.

"Keep to the right," I said, "and let the trucks and big stuff go by and we'll be fine." Estelle gave me a dirty look, but she took my advice. We sailed along at about thirty-five in a nice controlled way. Up ahead was a bridge overpass. Someone had written on it in big red letters.

MONDAY I LOVE YOU, it said.

I shuddered, as if someone had walked on my grave. I could feel goose bumps crawl up and down my spine. I felt the way I do when I read a line of poetry, or a sudden, beautiful truth. A revelation. Just when I thought I had them licked, tears coursed their way down my cheeks, as if they knew the way.

Estelle slowed to a snail's pace.

"What now?" she asked. "You want me to stop? Pull over? Are you sick?"

I shook my head, sending drops flying. "No, it's nothing. Only what someone wrote on the underpass. It's silly. Very silly."

Estelle pulled into a Texaco station and stopped. "It makes me very nervous driving when you're like that," she said, biting her lip. "Maybe I ought to take you to the emergency room. Maybe they could give you a shot or something."

"I'm perfectly okay. It got to me, that's all. Did you see? It said, 'Monday I love you.' " I looked over at Estelle to see her reaction, not really expecting her to understand.

"At least it isn't dirty," she said. "Mostly they write pornography on those overpasses. My mother says in her day all they did was draw big hearts with arrows through them and you wrote your initials and the initials of the boy you were in love with. Nowadays it's all filth."

"Let's go," I said, suddenly itchy. "What're we waiting for?"

Estelle stared.

"Your eyes are all sunk in," she commented. "It must be due to all that crying." I could feel her waiting, expecting some sort of confession from me. I wasn't going to budge.

"My eyes are always sunk in," I said. "It runs in our family."

A gas-station attendant with "Eddie" written on his breast pocket came over to the car and knocked on the window. When Estelle rolled it down a crack, he said, "Whaddya say, girls? You want something? Gas? Oil? Air in your tires?"

"We're waiting for the rain to stop," Estelle said.

His eyebrows shot up. "You tried the windshield wipers? They do wonders with them these days."

In a huff, Estelle rolled up the window, almost nailing

Eddie's nose as she went. He jumped back in an exaggerated way and made an obscene gesture.

"See? See? What did I tell you?" Estelle pulled out into traffic without looking to see what was coming. Tires squealed, brakes screamed.

I put my hands over my eyes.

7

When I was little, before William was my friend, my mother made a career of taking me around to child model agencies, entering me in beauty contests. It was not beyond the realm of possibility that some important person would spy me and cry out, "That face! Perfect! Sign her up!" She'd read of such things happening. The child, me, Grace Schmitt, would earn such vast sums as to make it advisable, indeed necessary, to establish a trust fund. The breath caught in the throat, thinking of such things. A trust fund. The child would buy its parents the mansion that had always been out of reach. Mansion complete with Olympic-size swimming pool and Jacuzzi, though the parents would use neither, being unable to swim and afraid of swirling waters in the home. Like famous performers or rock stars who, though leading lives of total debauchery, were always good to the old folks, I would provide.

If I'd been older, I might've been embarrassed by such presumption. But what did I know? I was on the threshhold of five and going downhill all the while, though mercifully unaware of time's toll. Dressed in my little puffed sleeves, matching bloomers and black patent-leather ankle straps, off I'd go. In those days my father held a steady job and my mother took some time off and led the life of a typical carefree housewife. Our floors and windows were murky, the laundry piled up. My mother, despite her faults, has never been house proud.

Smelling strongly of bubble bath, I'd stand like a statue while my mother brushed my hair. Well, the hair was a problem. Full of static electricity, wispy, mouse brown, it lacked something. A blond, curly wig, made of real hair, was considered, discussed. And dismissed, the price prohibitive. So I went with the natural look, smiling, quite happy with my lot.

After each interview, my mother made a point of treating me to a black-and-white soda, my favorite, or a chocolate malted, hers. Malteds, though delicious, always made me feel sick. I would start out full of enthusiasm. Then, about halfway through, nausea would take hold. Even if I drank slowly, I couldn't avoid the sick feeling. My early childhood is full of memories of leaning over strange toilet bowls in ladies' rooms, dry heaving.

Once I was a runner up (fourth place) in a beauty contest sponsored by our local hardware store, where my father happened to be working at the time. The first prize was a snow shovel, I remember, won by a large, goofy-looking boy whose father was the president of the Chamber of Commerce. It was said by some that the boy was more than ten, the age limit for the contest entries, but no one wanted to go to the wall on this point. This was a small town, and most of the people worked locally.

For my trouble, I got a free packet of parsley seeds. We planted them in our tiny backyard when spring came. They never came up, and it wasn't until quite a lot later that we discovered we were supposed to have soaked the seeds in water before putting them in the ground.

But my mother was ecstatic. Set aflame by our victory, she batted at my father's morning paper, crying, "See! See! I knew it. We have a little beauty here. Right in our midst! Didn't I tell you? Yes, I certainly did." And from behind the shield of his newspaper, I caught one of my father's eyes surveying me. The eye was dubious. Was I indeed a beauty?

If something is said often enough, does it come true? My mirror did not lie. I wasn't beautiful but thought I was, for I'd been told so often. The myth had been planted and nourished.

Actually I resembled a baby bird, newly unseated from the nest, mouth constantly open for the passing worm. Hair impossible. Looking back at myself in those days, I smile at my own innocence. Children are so wise, so tender, so unsuspecting. So at the mercy of adults. As well as of other children less tender than themselves. I didn't know at the age of four what unhappiness was.

All these things happened before we moved out of our house on Lily Pond Lane. I loved that house, loved our backyard with its clothesline, the moth-eaten bag full of clothespins hanging from it. Loved watching my overalls and panties with ruffled behinds blowing in the wind. We never had a clothes dryer. My mother loved the smell of sun in the clothes, she said. Once, a neighbor helping her fold the clean clothes sniffed at them and said, "What is that wonderful smell? What did you put in your rinse water?" And my mother smiled pityingly and said, "Fresh air and sun." That's the stuff TV commercials are made of.

We had no dishwasher either, except for my father. When I got older, I helped wash and dry, but he was forever putting dishes back into the water, dishes I'd washed that emerged from the suds with bits and pieces of eaten food still on them. My father went into a rage when he discovered the cupboard bare of clean dishes. My mother never washed a dish if she could help it.

"It's a waste of time," she said gaily. "They'll only get dirty again."

When my father lost his job at the hardware store,

we moved out of that house. I was very sad and went around touching every bush, every twig, the clothesline and even our mailbox, which hung crooked and was painted the same pale blue as the house. It had a big 9 on it, but the number of the house was actually nineteen. When the 1 had blown off during a windstorm, we'd never thought to put it back.

The neighbors across the street, the ones with the big black Lab, hung out the flag the day we moved. I didn't know what it meant. I thought maybe it was a national holiday, like the Fourth of July or Memorial Day. But when I asked the girl who lived there, who loved her dog and dressed him in her old baby clothes and stuffed him into an ancient pram and even put mosquito netting over him as she trundled him up and down the driveway, why their flag was hanging out, she said snippily, "Because you're moving."

Our next house was an apartment. It was painted a horrid color, a mixture of gray and brown, both inside and out. Our landlord lived above us and was always snooping around, asking if there was anything he could do. My mother said, "Well, yes, Mr. Barry, if you'd fix the latch on the kitchen door, I'd appreciate it," and we never saw him up close again. Except for his footsteps climbing the outside stairs to where he lived, he might as well have died.

And if my father was late with the rent, as he often was, Mr. Barry stationed himself on the far side of the street and stayed there until my father finally sent me out with the cash in an old envelope with the stamp torn off. My father collected stamps in those days. We always paid our rent in cash.

I never liked a house as much as that Lily Pond Lane one though. I loved that house. No place we've lived since has meant so much to me. Maybe because that was the happiest time of my life. Either the house made me happy or I made the house happy. One or the other. Maybe a little of both. It was one of those perfect times that doesn't have or need an explanation. It just *was*, and I remember it with love and joy, and probably always will.

Some people eat supper in front of the TV. Other people, I've heard, actually talk to each other during the meal. In our house, my mother switches the radio on just as we sit down to eat. Those droning voices get on my nerves, but it's her house.

"When you have your own house, Grace," she says when I complain, "you can do what you like. But until then . . ." She smiles, twirling the dial.

So we listened as we ate our continental supper: fettucine Alfredo out of a box, green beans amandine out of the freezer.

"I always say what would we do without these frozen people." My mother never took her eyes off me as she crunched down on an amandine and winced, reminded of her recent root canal. "Would you believe, Grace, in the olden days, there was no such thing as frozen food. Can you believe it?"

I could and did, wondering about the Eskimos. My mother chewed every mouthful twenty times, as she'd heard this cut down on caloric intake and kept you thin. I couldn't help noticing that the constant movement of her jaws made her nose move too. She watched me, I watched her nose.

"You all right?" she asked for the fourth time.

I nodded.

"Sure? Maybe a laxative?"

She was always flushing me out.

"Why are your eyes so bloodshot, Grace?" A sudden, terrible idea occurred to her. I could see it travel across her face and hit her brain.

"You're not *on* anything, are you?" In her agitation, she put down her fork. "Coke? Heroin? Crack?" She knew all the words.

"Yeah, Ma," I said wearily, not having the strength to laugh, "I'm on 'em all."

"You can tell me, Grace. You can tell your mother. It's only a mother's duty to help her child." She leaned toward me, forehead creased with worry lines. "You can always confide in your mother, Grace. What's wrong? Something's wrong. I can always tell."

Why is it, I wondered, that people who can't handle their own problems, much less other people's, always want to know what's wrong?

51

"Nothing new," I told her. "All the same old stuff."

"You should get out more," she said brightly. "Go meet new people, make new friends. That way you'd be happier. You have to make an effort, Grace."

Suddenly the announcer's voice cut in. There'd been a shooting and robbery at the Amoco station out on the highway, he told us, breathless with excitement. I figured that local announcers didn't get too many chances at dishing out exciting stuff like this.

"Listen," my mother commanded, head tilted toward the radio as if that way she'd hear better. As if I wasn't listening. She loved stuff like shootings and robberies. I guess it was the only drama in her life.

The gas-station attendant was even at this very moment on his way to the hospital in the county ambulance, the announcer said, which had answered the call for help in a record time of three minutes and eight seconds.

"Well, I never." My mother's eyes darted around the room, checking for possible danger spots. She got up and pulled the curtains closer together. As if *he* was out there, thinking of breaking and entering our little home.

"We will keep you informed of any new developments," the announcer told us. "Stay tuned."

"I bet," I said.

When I finally escaped, I locked myself in my room and sat on my bed, looking down at myself. I threw out my chest suddenly, as far as it would go. Then I marched over to the mirror and began to strip. I stripped all the way down to my bras, which were still there, guarding the fortress, holding it in. I'd got the crazy idea that if I slept in my bras, I'd wake up and my breasts would be normal size. I needed to see myself as Ashley and the others had seen me. I wanted to know how bad it was.

Worse than I'd thought. I was a terrible, awesome sight. Even seen through slitted eyes, I knew I was ludicrous. Laughable. Once, when I was a lot younger, B.C. (Before Chest, as I thought of it), I went with my mother to a store where she tried on clothes in a communal dressing room. I remember laughing behind my hand at a woman with humongous breasts. No doubt she'd been aware of me and my amusement. More than once, I'd asked silently for the woman's forgiveness. Forgive me. I didn't know.

What on earth made me think wearing two bras might make me look smaller? All it did was push my flesh around, shoving me up and out. Bulges I'd never had before now bulged significantly. Bulges that, when pushed down, sprang up of their own accord.

A deep red wave of shame crept over me from waist to forehead. Above the billowing flesh my head looked small, inadequate, my face confused and pinched, as if I'd just been told I had a brain tumor. Or as if I'd been caught in a giant machine and pressed. My head looked flat on top. I was a mess.

This, then, was the sight that had greeted Ashley's probing hands and eyes. I threw myself down on the bed, pillow over my face to muffle my cries. She must've heard me anyway.

"Grace! Grace!" My mother's voice came through the keyhole. "Let me in." If I hadn't been so beside myself I might've put my mouth up against the keyhole and shouted, "Let me alone!" so loud it would injure her eardrum and make her stop. My mother was a keyhole person, always watching, calling through it. Just because I had my own room didn't mean I had privacy.

"I'm thinking," I called to her, making my voice sound normal. "I have this big essay I have to write, and it requires a lot of thinking."

"Oh," I heard her say.

I felt a sudden, sharp pain in my chest. Maybe I was having a heart attack. Maybe I was dying. I'd heard of people my age dying. A boy over in Clarksville died after being tackled in a football game. Doctors said he'd had a heart condition that no one knew about until they did an autopsy. Maybe I had a heart condition and was going to die at any moment. They'd lay me out and kids from school would come to the funeral, kids who despised me for the way I looked; kids like Ashley would come and cry loudly so they'd get noticed, then they'd embrace each other, hang on each other outside the church so people would look at them and say, "How sad. They loved Grace so."

I waited for another pain to strike. I waited quite a long time. Nothing happened. Finally I sat up and drew my knees up to my chest. I have fat knees, too. Like old ladies you see on buses with their fat knees spread apart to give balance and support. It's awful, having fat knees.

54

I considered eliminating Ashley. Wiping her off the face of the earth. Would it make me feel better? Recently I'd read about an ancient method of torture. It involved putting a person inside a bag of snakes and tying the bag so neither the person or the snakes could escape. I thought about that.

"Grace." The voice was at the keyhole again. I remained silent. Maybe she'd think I was asleep or so deep in thought I couldn't hear.

"Grace, it's the telephone."

I jumped to my feet, fat knees or no.

It was probably Estelle. Estelle was the only one who called me. "Is it Estelle?" I asked.

"No." My mother's voice sounded breathless. Excited.

"Well, who then?"

"It's a boy."

"A boy? Is that what you said, a boy?"

"Yes. A boy." I heard her uneven breathing.

Goose bumps marched up and down me, across, all over.

"What does he want?" I whispered through the keyhole.

"I didn't ask him. He said he wants to speak to Grace."

I put on my red-and-black plaid bathrobe and unlocked the door. My mother clasped her hands and watched me go, wordless, probably saying her prayers. Please, God, make it lovely. For Grace's sake, make it lovely. For mine.

"Hello," I said boldly into the telephone.

"Is this Grace Schmitt?"

"Yes."

"Well, this is Charlie."

The only Charlie was Charlie Oates, who was big and blond and sexy. A hunk.

"Charlie." My voice caught in my throat, choking off further words. Charlie Oates.

"Yes, Charlie. I was wondering if . . ." The voice came to a halt.

I almost hung up. I wanted to. I was almost sure it was somebody fooling around. I thought I heard noises in the background.

But I hung on, hoping against hope.

"I was wondering if you'd . . ." Again the voice stopped. "If you'd go to the dance with me Friday."

I swallowed and closed my eyes. Spots danced in my eyeballs. I blinked my eyes open. My mother hugged the wall, pale. Listening. Saying prayers. Please, God, please. Be nice. That's what she prayed.

"Dance?" I said, and my mother's face was consumed by joy.

"Yeah. There's this dance in the gym Friday. After the game."

"Friday. Tomorrow?"

"Yeah, that's right. Tomorrow."

I swallowed again and said, "All right."

"Wear your black . . ." Charlie said, and it was like canned laughter on TV. Ha ha ha ha ha ha ha, they laughed. Ha ha ha ha ha ha.

I slammed down the receiver. Too late I slammed it down. My mother huddled in the corner, clutching her unanswered prayers in her tightly clenched fists.

"It was a joke," I said in a loud, ragged voice. "It was all a big joke. I don't know why you're surprised. I certainly wasn't. The minute you said it was a boy, I knew it was a joke."

My mother and I stared at each other. She put her fist to her mouth. I smiled.

"I knew it all along," I told her. "He said he was Charlie Oates. He said he wanted me to go to the dance with him Friday in the gym after the game. It was like one of those teenage romances. Unreal. I hate those teenage romances. They make me sick. I have to go now. I have to think some more."

My mother put out her hand. I avoided looking at it. I studied a spot over her head.

"I have work to do," I said. Then I went into my room and locked my door. Somehow I didn't think she'd be at the keyhole again tonight.

I'd barely settled down when the telephone rang again. I could hear it through the thin walls. No, I thought despairingly. They wouldn't. Not twice in one night.

I heard my mother come tapping, like a wicked witch, or a ghost, seeking retribution. In a voice as penetrating as a stiletto, she said, "It's Ms. Govoni, Grace. She wants to speak to you."

"Tell her I'm dead!" I shouted. "Tell her I'm having a nervous breakdown. Tell her anything!"

"She says she wants to ask a favor of you."

If it really was Govoni, I thought, I owe her one. She'd been kind to me. I got up, unlocked my door and padded heavily past my mother.

"Hello," I said, my neck muscles so tight I could hardly turn my head. If it was another hoax, I planned to tear the telephone out by its roots and hurl it through the window where, by enormous good luck and more enormous coincidence, Ashley would happen to be walking by, and the telephone would nail her, causing permanent brain damage.

"Grace, it's Mary Govoni. Could you baby-sit Saturday? I have a lecture I don't want to miss, and my regular sitter just called to say she has the chicken pox. So I thought of you."

Why did you think of me? I wondered. Probably because you know I'm available, am always available. No wild parties for Grace. No bizarre teen behavior with the boys. Grace, the perfect, most reliable sitter. She even does the dishes.

I hate myself when I get like that. I hate me when I'm bitter. Even if I have good reason to be bitter.

I wondered if Ashley ever baby-sat.

I told her okay. It was the least I could do. For all I know, Govoni might be on my side.

I didn't even know she *had* kids.

9

William was my first real friend. He had a wide, flat forehead and a snub nose that was so small I wondered how he could breathe through it. When I asked him what he did when he had a cold, he only laughed and punched me. William had beautiful dark eyes. When my mother saw William, she said, "With those eyes, he'll be a heartbreaker someday." I didn't know what a heartbreaker was and imagined William hammering away at a box of heart-shaped candies, the cinnamon kind, which were my favorites.

That was the summer I was six. William was eight and big for his age. My father was a croupier at a casino in Atlantic City, New Jersey. It was a very responsible job, he said. He worked all night, and sometimes, if I woke early, I went outside and waited for him at the curb. He always took a cab home. He wore a black suit and a very white shirt and black patent-leather shoes just like mine. It was his job to keep an eye on the money at the gaming tables where people bet. Once he saw a man lose ten thousand dollars on one roll of the dice, he told me. Being a croupier was a very demanding job, he said. My mother and father and I rented a little gray cottage a few blocks from the beach. We heard the waves roll in and out and watched the lights from the Ferris wheel and listened to the gulls complain about the handouts they got. Gulls are very greedy and not really nice, though sometimes beautiful. Like some people I know.

Sand drifted into our clothes, our teeth, our hair. Under our front door. The smell of the sea fought with the smell of saltwater taffy. Sometimes when the wind rose and the tide with it, we'd walk down to the ocean to watch the waves.

William and I ran back and forth, getting as close to the water as we could without getting wet. William was a daredevil, much more so than me, and once he got caught and was dragged out, out farther than I could reach. I saw his arms sticking up, heard him call. I put my hands over my eyes and looked through my fingers at his head riding the waves. I was terrified. I tried to yell but my voice wouldn't work. An old man walking his dog waded in and took William by the hair and pulled him to the sand. Up ahead, our mothers, William's and mine, walked placidly on the boardwalk. They didn't turn their heads. They hadn't seen what had happened.

"You kids get back to where you come from," said the old man in an angry voice. His face looked yellow, and his narrow shoulders had big moles all over. He was breathing hard. His dog barked until he said, "Quiet, boy."

"Tell your mother to keep an eye on you or you might not be so lucky next time," the old man told us, and we ran away and didn't even thank him.

When William's mother scolded him for getting all wet, we looked at each other and didn't tell. It was our secret.

William and I vowed eternal friendship. We might've even if William hadn't been swept out to sea. We thought if we were eternal friends, we would help each other through life. We'd be blood brothers. That's what William said. First, though, he told me we'd have to cut ourselves and mix our blood together, and that would make us blood brothers and eternal friends.

"That's what some American Indians used to do," William said. I said I was scared of blood. He said it wouldn't bleed much. He got a shell from the beach and broke it into two sharp pieces with a rock. William said he'd do the cutting. I was scared of being hurt. He said it wouldn't hurt much.

"Put up your hand," he told me, so I did. The shell slashed across my skin like fire, and blood came out all over. He threw the piece of shell away.

"Suck it, suck it!" William yelled. I sucked as hard as

I could. Then William cut himself with his piece of shell, only it was a little cut, not big like mine.

It hurt, even though William said it wouldn't. It *did* hurt.

We held our hands over another, bigger shell that was shaped like a little dish and let our blood drip into it. William stirred our blood for a while, mixing it.

"Now we're blood brothers," William said.

Only mine wouldn't stop coming. We went inside to ask William's mother's boyfriend Alfie if he could stop my blood coming.

Alfie jumped out of his chair and hollered, "What goes on here? You crazy kid!" and I knew he meant William. Alfie bandaged my hand as best he could, and pretty soon it started leaking through the bandage, so Alfie put us in the car and took us to the emergency room at the hospital. They fixed us up there, both William and me, and the doctor wanted to know how we'd got the cuts. William said he was playing with a knife and it slipped and got me. And him too, though his cut was only little. William was a good liar. He always made up stories like that.

My cut turned out to be in the shape of a V. A big V. William's looked like a straight line. He was a little disappointed but not much.

"Now we're blood brothers," he told me. I had always wanted a brother and so didn't mind that it hurt, getting a brother. My mother and father said I better not play anymore with William. I said it wasn't his fault.

William's mother told fortunes in a gypsy tearoom. She was a Russian princess who escaped from Russia in a sleigh pulled by snow-white horses. William's father was a prince who was eaten by wolves. All this happened before William was born. When William's eyes got all wide and glistening, I knew he was making it up.

After the cutting, my mother didn't like William anymore. "He's too pretty for a boy . . . and too wild, cutting you like that. It's a disgrace."

William too pretty? How could that be? He was William. Everything he did astonished and delighted me. I had never had such a friend.

"What a beautiful child," I heard people say as William and I raced by, barefooted, hand in hand, in hot pursuit of sunshine and sea and saltwater taffy. "What a perfectly beautiful child."

At first, I stopped and smiled at them, thinking they spoke about both of us. William and me. Then I became aware that their faces turned toward William, away from me. They smiled at him, patted his rosy cheeks.

"He's my brother," I told them proudly. William swung my hand and grinned at me, nodding. "She's my sister," he said, pleased at our playacting. Then we spun in wide circles, and the sand hid between our toes and we were completely, utterly happy.

I won a straw hat at a penny pitching booth on the boardwalk that summer. It had a blue band and was too big for me. I had to keep my hand on it whenever I went walking. The wind from the ocean wanted that hat in the worst way. Every night I watched my father put on his black bow tie and suit. Then he'd brush his hair and put such a straight part in it it looked as if it was made with an ax. My father wore after-shave lotion that my mother said made him smell like a fruit. She didn't say what fruit. I sniffed at him and decided he smelled like a cherry, but William said he smelled more like an apple.

It was my best summer. I wished my father could've gone on being a croupier, but he was let go because business at the casino was down. That's what he said, anyway. William and I saw an old man skateboarding down the boardwalk. I thought it might be the same old man who'd rescued William, but William said it wasn't. The man who rescued him, William said, had yellow hair and wore two big gold rings on each hand. I think he was wrong. We waited to see if the man on the skateboard would stop so we could see if he had gold rings on as well as yellow hair, but he just kept moving fast, until one day he tripped over a runaway cat and went flying and broke all his bones and never went skateboarding again. We heard all sorts of stories.

My cut finally healed. I had a big V right where my thumb went out. William didn't have anything. His cut was all gone. He was very sad about that. He said he'd send me a postcard. William and his mother and Alfie were going to try their luck in Florida. My mother wrote our address down on a piece of paper, which I gave to William. But I never heard from him.

It was that summer of my friendship with William that made me half conscious of the fact that I was not an appealing child. I knew that from the way they looked at William, their faces all open and joyful, and the way they looked at me.

I tried. God knows I tried. But even with ribbons plaited in my newly washed hair, a smile on my face and red sandals my mother bought me on my feet, I lacked the special quality that makes a child appealing. Over the years, I told myself, things might change, I might develop this quality; but now I know this is not so. Nor will it ever be.

I am the sort who's always chosen last, the wallflower, though I do not dance. In this life there are winners and losers. I'm a loser. If I could do anything to change this, I would. But I am powerless. There is nothing to do but accept it and get on with my life.

10

In the morning my head felt as if it was filled with rocks. My eyes seemed stuck together with Scotch tape, my face as sticky as if I'd eaten a Hershey bar while I was sleeping. I considered playing dead. You read about people having little strokes, little heart attacks no one even knows they've had until their personality changes drastically. Or they start mumbling and can't even remember their own name. Or what day of the week it is, or even the year. Or they forget words for simple things, like "fork" or "soap."

I'd read about a disease that makes people age prematurely. There were pictures showing ten-year-olds who looked like senior citizens. Or twelve-year-olds who looked in their eighties. It was terrible, tragic. I decided maybe that's what ailed me. There was nothing young or charming or spirited about me. I might as well be a hundred as fifteen. I walked old, talked old, thought old.

I ran my hands over my face, searching for wrinkles; big dark moles sprung up in the night when my eyes were closed. Sunken cheeks on account of my teeth were all gone. The only part of me that might pass for young was my mouth. I had a really nice mouth. Even I had to admit that. It was well shaped and sort of curly at the ends. And naturally red. When I smiled, my mother kept telling me, I had a glow. Estelle said she thought my ears were nicer than my mouth. Estelle and I sometimes dissected each other, good points against bad. I told Estelle she had nice hair. Privately I thought if Estelle's mother didn't lay off with the elaborate hairdos, Estelle was headed for trouble.

There weren't enough good points between me and Estelle combined, though, to make one halfway decent-looking person. That was the truth of it.

"Grace." My mother breathed through the keyhole. "Time to get up."

I made a noise so she'd know I'd heard. Suppose I said I wasn't going to get up? Suppose I said I was afraid to leave the house? That from here on in I was housebound. Agoraphobia, they call it. Fear of open spaces. A terrible thing and very real. Lots of people, I'd read, suffered from it. There didn't seem to be any cure. If you had agoraphobia, you sat in your house all day huddled in a shawl, peering from behind the curtains at the postman, the United Parcel truck, the paperboy who always threw the paper under the hedge or into the neighbor's yard. You got somebody to go to the grocery store to get your groceries. You got a friend to take your books back to the library and get out some more books. They were never books you cared about reading, but you were in no position to be choosy. You were anchored to your house forever more.

I tried to imagine what it would be like. I would never have to go to school again, never have to see Ashley or Charlie Oates. They'd send home my lessons and my exams, and I'd never have to go to the girls' room again. Never be shoved and whispered at by a ferret-faced little creep in a black leather jacket who never had a girl so much as say hi to him. No more fat mama stuff for me.

Estelle would come to report the school news to me when she brought my homework over. Dr. Gleason would have to come to the house to fill my teeth. My mother would trudge over to Ware's and buy me a pair of jeans from the women's department where they specialized in large sizes. And she'd splurge and buy me two pairs of pink panties with elastic around the waist and legs, panties that when I took them off you could still see where they'd been on account of the elastic tracks printed on my flesh.

I lay very still, watching my chest move up and down, wondering if it was possible to turn my life around. The way they keep telling you. Make Your Life Happen.

Gain Control of Your Life. This Is the First Day of the Rest of Your Life. Blah, blah, blah.

"Grace. Dear. It's getting late."

If I sealed off my keyhole, how would my mother and I communicate? Maybe we'd write each other notes, which we'd leave on the kitchen table. And when my father came home from time to time, he'd read them silently, stooping a little over the table, looking over his shoulder now and then as if he was doing something secret and forbidden.

If I never left the house, I decided, I'd be as good as dead. Which wouldn't be a tremendous change from what I was right now. Still, there were certain things— flowers, the look of the sky when it was filled with clumps of little clouds bundled together in one corner, like sheep in a pasture. Children, the way they move, the way their mittens dangle at the end of strings stuffed up their sleeves. I wouldn't want never to go outside. It would be very boring, for one thing.

I got out of bed slowly, and padded over to the mirror, a glutton for punishment. Avoiding a full-face confrontation, I turned sideways and looked at myself over my shoulder.

Sometimes I'm so gross I even gross myself out.

When I arrived at the breakfast table the radio was still on. Had it been on all night, I wondered? My mother listened intently to the rehash the announcer was dishing out, as if she were hearing it for the first time.

69

"This man is probably armed and considered dangerous," the announcer said excitedly. "He is thought to be the same man who escaped from the state prison over in Torry last week and is now wanted for questioning in connection with the assault and attempted rape of two high school girls in Crawford county last year. Police have issued a warning to all citizens against opening their doors to strangers, as well as against picking up hitchhikers. The man is a white male, six feet tall, in his late teens or early twenties, wearing blue jeans and cowboy boots. He has black hair and a mustache. He is, I repeat, thought to be armed and dangerous."

"Those guys give me a pain," I said. "They think they're Laurence Olivier or something. How about the poor guy at the gas station? How's he doing?"

As if he'd heard me and was answering, the announcer said solemnly, "The gas-station attendant was taken to Overland Hospital, where he is reported to be in critical condition."

"Well." My mother's eyes sparkled. "Who would think? Right in our own backyard. You never know. Things that go on." She shook her head. Then, "Why don't you wear that pretty blue blouse I bought you?" she asked me, and I knew from the way her eyes narrowed at me that she hated my Hawaiian print shirt with the long tails that hung out and concealed a good part of me. Tough. I was the one who was wearing it, not her.

When the telephone rang, I jumped. My mother stayed where she was.

70

"Answer it, will you, Grace? My hands are all wet," she said, running her hands under the cold water. I shook my head. She let it ring some more, then grabbed up the receiver and said "Yes?" into it in a feisty way.

"May I ask who's calling?" she said. Who did she think she was anyway, an executive secretary?

"It's that Doris Brown." She held out the receiver. "I wish she wouldn't call so early in the morning. Mornings are so frantic around here."

I looked around our kitchen. It seemed pretty calm to me.

"Hello, Doris," I said, holding the receiver a little away from myself, in case it wasn't really Doris but someone masquerading as Doris.

"Grace. Can you sit tonight? Sorry for short notice. Got to get away for some R and R. Hope you're not busy."

Over the telephone Doris talked in shorthand. The thing I liked about her was she always called at the last minute, always apologized for doing so and always said, "Hope you're not busy." As if I ever was. I loved Doris for saying that.

I said five-thirty would be fine. "Plan to spend the night." She always said that too. "I'll probably be late. May spend the night with my girl friend. You know how it is."

"Sure," I said, not knowing how it was but willing to buy anything Doris said.

"Peachy," said Doris, signing off.

"She wants me to sit tonight," I told my mother. "I'll spend the night, because she's going to be very late." Well, I sure was in demand as a baby-sitter, anyway, I thought. First Govoni, now Doris.

My mother screwed up her face so she looked as if she might be hurting.

"I don't like you sitting off there, no neighbors or anything, alone and all," she said. "And now this," she waved at the radio. "This wild man on the loose. God knows what he's capable of. Anything. Everything. Most likely he's a pervert, too." She chewed her lip excitedly. "He's probably spaced out of his mind, snorting cocaine or something. You really shouldn't be alone out there. It's dangerous." My mother willed me to look at her.

I refused. As a matter of fact, I had been scared badly once or twice while baby-sitting at the Browns', by strange noises outside or loud bangs from a passing car, sounds that sounded like gunshots. But I'd have to be put on a rack to admit that to her now. One word of apprehension from me, and my mother would say, "Call her up and tell her I said NO." And I liked baby-sitting for Buster Brown. I liked the money I earned too. So I kept quiet and smiled patronizingly at my mother's anxieties.

"I won't be alone. The baby will be with me. We might play some cards." I should've known better than to joke with my mother. She has no sense of humor. None at all. Her lips never even twitched.

"You never know. I don't like it. You're too young to be out there all night by yourself."

She never listened to me. Nobody did. I shrugged and got out the vinyl overnight bag my father had won in a crap game. He won the strangest things. Once he brought home a roasting chicken he said he'd won in a poker game.

I had no intention of going to school. I planned to go to the library, wait for the doors to open, then sit down at one of the big, shiny tables, take out my yellow lined pad and a handful of sharpened pencils and go to work. If anyone asked, I'd say I was working on a school project. Lots of research was needed. Mrs. Quick, the librarian, was kind to me. To others, she was curt and brisk, but once she'd asked me if I'd got a good mark on my last paper, and did I want a cup of tea.

I put my nightgown into the bag, as well as my toothbrush and my Ace bandage. Sometimes, when I had a free moment, I practiced binding myself with the bandage. The way they did in the nineteen twenties. When bosoms were out and the fashion was to be flat chested. So women bound their breasts the way Chinese women bound their feet, so they'd be small and useless.

I'd discovered it was difficult to bind yourself. But there was no one I could ask to help. If I asked Estelle, she'd let it slip. "Grace Schmitt binds her boobs with an Ace bandage," Estelle would say to anyone who'd listen. Loose lips sink ships, Estelle. Keep your big blabbermouth shut, why don't you. But Estelle couldn't. She was incapable of keeping her mouth shut. And, as she was my only friend, I'd have to learn to bind myself.

I put my sunglasses in my pocket. I'd bought the biggest, roundest sunglasses I could find. They covered half my face. I liked to think they made me invisible. If you can't see a person's eyes, you can't really see the person. The lenses were pale blue. I hoped they lent me an air of mystery, as if I were a big superstar or a photojournalist.

"I'm off," I said. "See you tomorrow."

Fuzzy slippers slapping as she crossed to the sink, my mother didn't answer. I let myself out and stood quietly behind some bushes as the school bus stopped for pickup and thundered past. Then I set out, walking purposefully. I tried to walk as if I was thin; feet stepping high, stomach in, shoulders back. Light as a feather. There are always ways to deceive yourself.

A red Subaru pulled up beside me. I knew it was Govoni. I didn't feel like talking to anybody, but I had to stop. It would've been rude not to.

"Hop in," Ms. Govoni said. "I'm going your way."

"I'm headed for the library," I said, feeling blood rush to my face. "I have this paper I have to write. And research. I'm not going to school today." If she didn't like it, she could lump it, I decided.

"Okay. I'll drop you off there, then." She patted the seat. "Just push the mess out of your way." The seat was littered with candy wrappers, broken crayons and some plastic ears and noses from Mr. Potato Head. It probably was like that the other time I'd been in the car, but I hadn't noticed.

"It wouldn't take a detective to decide there were kids in this family," Ms. Govoni said. "They leave their trademarks everywhere."

"I didn't know you had a kid," I said. "Until you called, that is."

"Two," she said. "A boy and a girl."

"That's nice." What about the stories that said Ms. Govoni liked girls better than boys?

"Which do you like better?" I asked. "Girls or boys?"

"It's a toss-up," she said. "They're both young and pesky. When they get older and much peskier, maybe I'll make up my mind. It's nice having both."

It wasn't like driving with Estelle. Ms. Govoni kept her eyes on the road at all times, except when we were stopped at a red light.

"I'm glad I ran into you, Grace," Ms. Govoni said, frowning at her windshield. "I expect you're going through a bad patch right now." Little did she know.

"I've been through some myself. It's no fun. But I'll put my money on you. You'll survive, maybe even be stronger because of it. If you want to talk, remember, I'm a good listener. Best thing about me is, I never tell. My mother used to call me old zipper mouth."

We pulled up in front of the library. She turned to look at me, and I noticed how dark and kind her eyes were. How filled with compassion they were. Then, be-

75

cause I was embarrassed, because of what she knew about me, what I'd told her about Ashley in the girls' room, I said, to fill the empty space with words, "What does your husband do?"

Asinine question.

"I don't have one," she said.

"Oh." Again I felt the blood rush to my face. "Well. Thanks for the ride. I'm sorry."

"Don't be. I'm not. Remember." She grinned and looked younger, and I thought she probably didn't grin often. "Tell it to old zipper mouth and you can't go wrong. See you tomorrow, then. Thanks, Grace."

I got out and stood on the sidewalk, watching her battered little wagon pull out into traffic.

A bad patch. I wondered what a good patch was like. Wondered if I'd ever know.

Thanks for what?

11

When I was ten, just before I started getting breasts, my mother left home. It wasn't the first time and it probably won't be the last. It's the time I remember the best, though.

"She'll be back, hon. You wait and see. I know her. She'll be back before you can say Jack Robinson. Don't you worry." As he spoke, my father's foot moved agitatedly, keeping time with his words. "Ladies sometimes have to spread their wings, see if they can still fly. Take off." He winked at me and I turned my eyes away from his long, sad face.

"She left me," I said. "I bet it was because I didn't wash the dishes. Three times in a row I didn't wash them. That's what did it. She left me and she's never coming back."

"No," my father corrected me. "She left *me*. She didn't want to leave you behind, but I wouldn't let her take you. I said, 'Let Grace stay with me.' So she did."

I was pretty sure he was lying. That didn't sound like her, letting him talk her out of something. Usually, when my mother wanted to do something, she went ahead and did it. My father hardly ever opposed her. And even though I suspected my father of lying, I was impressed by his boldness and relieved to hear him say he wouldn't let her take me away with her.

Fortunately, at that time my father was between jobs. He did the cooking and cleaning and even took our clothes to the Laundromat and ironed my skirts and blouses for me so I always had clean, pressed clothes to wear to school. Which wasn't always the case when my mother was in charge.

He was a pretty good ironer and an even better cook. We had fried chicken and corn pudding and gingerbread from scratch. With whipped cream. We were pretty happy. My father let me stay home from school quite a lot. To keep him company, he said. I think he was lonely. We laid out a jigsaw puzzle on the card table. Whenever one of us passed by, we'd put in a bit of blue sky or maybe part of a red cape, until we'd finished with it. My father taught me to do the soft shoe, which is a dance like a tap dance only without tap shoes. While I danced, he kept time with his harmonica. Before my mother left,

I never knew he knew how to play the harmonica. It made him seem younger, somehow, jauntier. He'd been a mechanic and a seaman and a Ford auto worker. He'd been to Hong Kong and Tokyo, and he knew how to blow out the inside of an egg to make a Christmas tree ornament out of it.

Once he'd worked on a farm, he said. "And if I had my druthers, Grace," he told me, "I'd stick to the earth. Nothing like the land. Hard work, yes, but very satisfying. Nothing like it. Trouble is, you have to get up mighty early. That's the only bad part. You know me, Gracie. I like my shut-eye."

He answered a newspaper ad and, to our surprise, landed a job selling encyclopedias.

"Wouldn't you know. With your mother away, I had to land a plum job like this one." He always said my mother was "away" rather than "gone." I guess that comforted him, making believe she was sunning herself in Florida or off in New York City, seeing the sights. "Can't take it, Grace," he said. And when I asked why not, his mouth turned down, giving him a mournful look, and he said, "I can't leave you to fend for yourself, hon. No ifs or buts about it."

"Take me with you," I begged. "I won't be any trouble." I pictured us traveling the roads, sleeping under hedges at night, in stacks of hay, eating bread and cheese by the side of a rippling brook. Oh, it would be wonderful, I told myself. While my father was out selling encyclopedias, I'd keep house in a cave. Or a tent. And when we felt like moving on, we'd move on. My father canceled my plans, however. Instead, he arranged for me to spend the summer with my aunt Rena, the same Rena who gave juicy kisses at the Gathering of the Schmitt Clan. He told his sister Rena that my mother had to go out west to take care of her ailing sister. Aunt Rena said she didn't know my mother had a sister. My mother's family had never been friendly with my father's family, so my father said, sure, you remember her sister, the one with pigeon toes. My aunt Rena was none too proud of her failing memory, so she quit arguing and said I could stay if I was willing to work for my room and board.

Rena had had a husband once but he got away. She made me wash twice a week and go to church with her every Sunday. I had a little room up under the eaves in her farmhouse. Oh, but it was boiling hot that summer. I didn't mind. From my window I had a view of the valley and the cows that more than made up for the heat. I helped feed the hogs and chickens, and Aunt Rena taught me how to milk a cow. It was something, all right. Shooting that little stream of warm milk fresh from the cow's udder, sometimes shooting it square into my mouth. I liked everything about that farm, that summer, even though Rena was a tough lady. She was always after me about something. Scrub the tub, take out the garbage, cut your toenails. No wonder Rena's husband got away.

I couldn't take my eyes off Aunt Rena's elbows. From the back, with the sleeves of her checked shirt rolled up well so she could drive the tractor better, her elbows looked like the faces of little gnarled people. There was so much skin rippling around Aunt Rena's elbows, it tucked and folded itself into funny little mouths and ears and noses. I couldn't get over it. I made it a habit to ride directly behind her in the tractor so I could keep an eye on her elbows and watch the faces change expression when Rena shifted into first or slammed on the brakes. It was better than a puppet show.

My father came several times that summer, on the way from one place to another. He liked his job selling encyclopedias, but he said people weren't up to buying a whole lot. Money was tight.

"Never known it to be loose," Aunt Rena said, sniffing. "Heard from Grace, Frank? How's her sister doing? Seems like she's been gone a long time. The child misses her mother. Don't you, Grace?" and Aunt Rena's eye fixed on me, an event I always dreaded. I thought Rena's eyes could see through me, into my head, knew what I was thinking. It was eerie.

"Seems like there's more here than meets the eye." And Rena's eye went to my father. I went outside to see if a storm was coming. I'd got really good at reading clouds that summer. Besides, I didn't want to be there when my father was quizzed. Sooner or later Rena'd get the straight goods out of him. I wondered where my mother was, if she was thinking about us. But it was amazing how little I missed her. Living on the farm was fun. There was so much to do, so many animals to tend to, so much nature. Nature can be very absorbing, I found, once you get used to it. Once you know something about it.

There was a boy named Eric, a hired hand, Aunt Rena called him, who helped out with the heavy work. He had broad shoulders and blond hair, and he was sort of cute. He lived up the road from our farm. He was fourteen, and though he didn't talk much, he liked me. I could tell. Aunt Rena must've been able to tell too. "You stay away from that Eric," she warned. "He's too old for you. Don't think I don't see him giving you the eye. While you're under my roof, you do as I say, Grace. There'll be no shenanigans around here, mark my word." Aunt Rena talked like a character out of a book. Or an old movie. What kind of a word was "shenanigans," anyway? If Aunt Rena had had a dictionary I would've looked it up. As it was, I had to use my imagination. The way her lip curled when she said it meant it was another word for "no good." Eric was a no-good person, then. Was that what she'd meant? No he wasn't. Any fool could see he was a hard worker, industrious, eager to earn a buck. Eric ate his lunch out of a brown bag while sitting propped up by the warm wall of the barn. I went out to keep him company, talk to him. Well, the truth of it was, I talked, he listened. I told him all sorts of stories—where I'd been, what sights I'd seen. Eric only nodded, dipping his yellow head down into his lunch bag, seeing what he'd overlooked, eyes shining with excitement. He believed every word I said. I soon saw that, and it gave me a feeling of power. He was shy and seemed younger than me, although as I said, he was four years older. He'd never been anyplace, it seemed. When I told him about my father being a croupier—I made it sound like that's what he was doing now, leaving out the part about being an encyclopedia salesman, thinking that was a job that lacked glamor—Eric's eyes got very round.

"I sure would like to go to one of them casinos," he said. "Them gambling places. I saw it on TV. They stay open twenty-four hours a day. All night long. They never close doors. Any time of the day or night suits you, you just go inside there and lay your money down. Go on," he urged. "Tell me more."

I was flattered, never having had such an avid audience in my grasp before. I went wild, made up lots of stuff, just the way William used to do—things that never happened but might've if given a chance. Eric loved it all. If Aunt Rena hadn't crept up on us and yelled, "Time's a-wasting!" the way she did, we'd be there still, lollygagging around. That was another of Aunt Rena's words, "lollygagging." She was a pistol when it came to words, all right.

One day in mid-August, my father came trudging up the hill. I'd been picking peaches all morning for Aunt Rena to make into jam and preserves, and my arms and hands were all sticky. If you're not quick, and don't lick it off fast, the juice runs all over.

"How's my girl?" my father said, hugging me. "Happy? Say"—he held me at arm's length, studying me—"you're

83

all grown-up. While my back was turned, you grew up. How's Rena? Treating you all right?" The grooves at either side of his mouth looked so deep I could've laid my finger inside them, but otherwise he seemed all right. I didn't mention my mother. I figured if he'd heard from her, he'd say so.

Aunt Rena made my father go to church with us on Sunday. "How do you expect a child to have religion if her father sets a bad example, Frank?" she stormed. Aunt Rena was known for her temper, but I'd never seen it in action until then. Her face turned pale purple and the veins in her neck stood out so's you could practically reach out and grab one. My father always knew when he was licked. He came quietly, hat in hand. I wore my first pair of earrings, which I'd bought with money Aunt Rena had given me for helping her out. They were white plastic circles almost as big as a small plate and they dragged my earlobes down some, but I thought they were wonderful and made me look very grown-up. During the sermon, one of my earrings dropped off and made a pinging sound on the church floor. I scrabbled around under the pew looking for it until Aunt Rena hauled me up by my belt, glaring at me so I knew I'd better wait until church was over before I continued my search. After the last hymn, I found it and screwed it on tight so it wouldn't pop off again.

When we filed down the aisle and out into the sunlight, the first person I saw was Eric. He came right up to me and said, "I like your ear bobs."

"What?" I said. "What'd you say?"

He pointed. "I like them ear bobs," he repeated.

Well, that caused us to break up then and there. I have never heard such English in my life. I couldn't respect somebody who said "ear bobs" for "earrings." I was a snob, I know, but I couldn't help it. Shortly after, school started and Eric took the bus to the regional high school over in Clayton and I never laid eyes on him again.

Right after Eric and I broke up, so to speak, my father and I went back to Hoboken, where we came from. He said I had to start school too, though I would've been quite happy without it. Aunt Rena was sad I was leaving and threatened to enfold me in her massive arms and embrace and kiss me, but I skinned out of reach and she had to be content with a handshake. Aunt Rena was all right. I just couldn't face her spitty kisses.

We got home on a Tuesday and were just sitting down to supper when my mother trailed up the front walk, dragging her suitcase in one hand like it was filled with rocks, and dangling her high-heel shoes in the other.

"Whew," she said in greeting, "doesn't get much hotter 'n this, does it! September's always the hottest month." We were having corned beef hash. She said she'd have some. She chatted about this and that, and when my father said at last, "Where you been, Grace?" she only let her long red fingernails trail across the back of his neck and said, "Here and there, Frank, here and there. But home's best."

Oh no you don't, I thought. You're not getting away

with that, not that easily. Not after what you did. You tell us where you were, what made you go off like that, leaving me and him and not telling us where you went, what you did. You have to explain.

I looked at my father. I wanted him to demand an explanation in a cold, hard voice, wanted him to tell her we'd done fine without her, she could just take her shoes and suitcase and go back to where she'd been. But I knew he wouldn't say any of it. One look at his face and I knew he was dying from love, from happiness that she'd come back. That was all that mattered. To him. Inside, I was so angry, so clogged with rage, I could hardly speak. They wouldn't have heard me anyway. They had eyes and ears only for each other.

I hung around, cleared the table, expecting at any moment she'd say she was sorry. I opened my mouth once or twice to demand an apology, but each time, I closed it without making a sound. The words wouldn't come. I wanted to hit her. I ached to hit her, smack the smile off her face.

How dare she just come back and act as if nothing had happened! How dare she!

"I'm sorry. I'll never do it again." Those were the words I wanted to hear. I ached to have her put her arms around me and say, "You're my own little girl, Grace. I missed you. I'm sorry I went off and hurt you so."

But she was silent and so was I.

12

Doris lived in a trailer out on Old Town Road. Kenny gave her the trailer as a wedding present, she said. She would've preferred a set of china, maybe with some place settings of silver thrown in, but he had his heart set on living in a trailer. When he got out of the Navy, that is. Kenny was stationed in Tokyo, Japan, at the present. Had been for a while. He had to leave for Tokyo when the baby was only about two months old. Doris said she'd almost gone crazy for a few weeks after he left. Then she landed a job at the Bureau of Motor Vehicles and that set her up, got her out of the house. She just put the baby in the day-care center and took off for work.

Her job at the Bureau of Motor Vehicles makes Doris

bad tempered, she said. Everyone at the bureau is bad tempered. They don't get jobs there if they're not. Doris smiled when she told me these things so I'd know she was only joking. Doris pays me fifteen dollars when I stay with the baby overnight. I count on that fifteen dollars. I bank every penny. Every time I sit with that little baby, I figure I'm that much closer to getting my chest operation.

Doris's trailer is very colorful inside. It's all orange; there's an orange shag rug, an orange pullout couch and orange-and-brown curtains. Doris even has orange towels in the bathroom and orange linoleum in the kitchen. She took a decorating course once, she said, and fell in love with orange. Besides, she learned in the decorating course that if you live in a small place, the best thing to do is have everything the same color. That way, the place looks bigger.

"Fix yourself a Coke, Grace, anything you want," Doris told me before she went to take her shower. I put Buster in his high chair and got his dinner ready.

It's no big deal. He gets dried cereal mixed with milk. Then, for dessert, I give him apple sauce or apricots or pears. He gobbles it all up. What does he care if it looks like throw up? Buster's not a picky eater. He usually tries to grab hold of the spoon and feed himself. I think he's very advanced. Once I let him have the spoon, and he stuffed his nose and ears with gunk. He was a mess.

While Buster gummed his food, I thought about Ashley and the others in the girls' room. I tried not to dwell on it too much, but it was hard not to. It ate at me. I had a tremendous desire to get even, but more than that, I had a lot of hate in my heart. I'm amazed at how much. I know it's bad and destructive, that it drags me down and leaves Ashley untouched. In one fell swoop, she'd done me more harm than I could do to her in a million years.

Why had she singled *me* out? Was it simply my appearance, or was it because I was a nobody, an unpopular girl with no personality and no looks and no friends to speak of? An object of fun.

Or was it because she had no conscience or remorse. There are such people in the world. When they lead a convicted mass killer of babies and small children to the electric chair, news reports often say, "He showed no remorse."

Was that Ashley? Was she incapable of human feeling? Would she go through life mowing people down, one way or the other, and remain untouched, like the guys in charge of the ovens at Dachau and Auschwitz?

"Whaddya think?" Doris startled me, brought me back to here and now. "This"—she held up a red dress—"or this"—she indicated a plaid pant suit. I told her either would be great. Doris is a compulsive shopper. She can't go into a store without buying something, even if it's only a pair of panty hose.

"It's just a bunch of us girls," Doris told me, frowning, trying to decide. "Who cares what I wear, right? It's not like I'm going to a fancy-dress ball where all the guys wear tuxes and all. All it is is me and Linda and Maura and maybe Tara. Well, Tara now." Doris jabbed her finger at me, making her eyes wide. "She's something else. When she's around, the men are too. Tara's getting a divorce. She's the kind has to have the whole joint hanging on her, cozying up to her. Tara's bad news. But the boys love her. She's thirty miles of bad road. That's what Kenny says, thirty miles of bad road."

"There's a girl in my school like that," I said. "Her name's Ashley."

"Ashley!" Doris cried. "First we got Tara, now it's Ashley. It's *Gone With the Wind* night around here, right?"

"I guess." Tara, and Ashley Wilkes. Except that Ashley was a man's name. Too much. "How come there's no Grace Schmitt in *Gone With the Wind*?" I asked Doris. She broke up at that.

"Hope your pal Ashley doesn't bear any resemblance to Leslie Howard," Doris joked. "I mean, he's cute and all, but he's not exactly what you might call sexy."

"Ashley's not my pal, Doris. I hate her. She's one of those perfect ones, the kind who looks like butter wouldn't melt in her mouth. Basically, though, she's a creep. A total rat." I could feel myself getting upset all over again, just talking about her, saying her name. "The boys fall all over themselves when she walks by. She's head of everything, boss lady of the school. If you saw her, you'd know what I'm talking about. She's too much—clothes, figure, the works. Just too much." I couldn't seem to stop talking.

Buster started making fussy noises, so I took him out of his high chair and let him crawl around.

"She does such mean things. She should be punished, but that kind never gets punished, I guess."

Then, to my astonishment and chagrin, I burst into tears. Doris looked dismayed. "Oh sweetie, don't," she said, patting me. "Don't. She's not worth it. Whatever she did to you, she's not worth getting yourself in a state about."

"I know, I know," I blubbered. "It's ridiculous. She's so bad, though. If I told you some of the things she did, you'd flip out, Doris. Truly. You'd absolutely flip out. It's not fair. People like her get it all. It's just not fair," I wailed. Doris handed me a tissue. I blew my nose. Buster put his little hand on the cupboard door where Doris kept the cookies and said, "Please." Clear as a bell it was. Please.

"Did you hear that!" Doris grinned. "The kid *can* talk. How about that!" Then both Doris and I clapped and carried on, and Doris put her fingers in her mouth and produced a piercing whistle, a whistle that could be heard for miles. Buster broke into tears.

"Oh Lord." Doris picked him up and soothed him. "First you, now him, Grace. What goes on here anyway?"

"Don't worry, we'll be fine. Have a good time," I said. "And drive carefully and don't do anything I wouldn't do." People always said that, and it sounded sort of cute, I thought. But coming from me, it sounded dumb. I wished I'd kept my mouth shut.

Doris put on her coat. "Lock the doors and turn the heat down when you go to bed," she told me, "and don't put beans in your noses. My mother always told us that. So once when she was gone, I did put beans in my nose, just stuffed some right up there, and my sister had to call the doctor and there was hell to pay."

I held Buster up to the window so he could watch her drive away. He waved at the car as it headed down the driveway and pulled out into the main road. I sang to him then, a little song I made up, and his little eyes were so bright and alert. I walked around the place, showing him things, telling him the names of stuff so he'd talk, really talk, soon and everyone would say how smart he was. I liked cuddling that little baby. He's so soft and warm. When I held him close and whispered secrets in his ear, he comforted me. I pretended he was my baby.

What harm did it do? I knew Doris wouldn't mind.

Besides, holding him eased the hate and the hurt a little. Not much, only a little.

13

It took me a while to come to grips with the fact that my parents had no social life, didn't seem to have any friends. I'd noticed other people's parents went places Saturday night—to the movies, maybe, or bowling, to a bar and grill, or perhaps dancing. The mother changed into her best clothes, dabbed perfume behind her ears while the father went to pick up the baby-sitter, or they left the kids alone if the oldest was old enough to keep the others from killing each other. There was a general exodus Saturday night, I'd observed, as I watched the red taillights go down the street, then turn right or left and disappear.

"Why don't you ever go out?"

"How come you don't have parties?"

"Why don't you have any fun?"

These were the questions I asked.

"Fun costs money," my father explained.

"Parties are expensive and a lot of work," said my mother, lips tucked neatly in upon each other.

Somewhere along in third grade, I think it was, we moved to a house on a street where all the houses resembled each other. Just as all the Schmitts resembled each other slightly. Something about the jaw line, the way the bushy eyebrows tilted up at the corners, lending a sinister air to the long, thin Schmitt faces.

I didn't resemble anybody. No one laid claim to my looks. No one took any responsibility.

All the houses on our street had windows a little too close together, as well as vestibules. I'd never heard of a vestibule before we moved to that house. My mother said, "I've always wanted a vestibule," and my father paid two months' rent in advance. It was one of our better times.

A vestibule is a little room you go into when you open the front door. It's not a hall, it's a vestibule, and it has a closet so you can hang up your coat and kick off your galoshes in it before you go into the living room.

"A vestibule," my mother told me, "is class. Real class." I believed her. She knew about such things and I didn't.

After we'd lived there awhile, it occurred to me to visit our next-door neighbors.

"You'll notice no one came to call," my mother said

94

bitterly. "You'll notice there were no casseroles, no homemade pastries that first night. These are not people who welcome newcomers."

I decided to do something about that. I'd noticed that a boy slightly older than me was riding his bicycle up and down his driveway next door. He never went out into the street. I didn't have a bicycle, but I had ridden one once or twice, so I decided to make the first move.

I went over and said hello.

"Hello," I said. Either he was deaf or didn't have any manners. Or, most likely, didn't want to get to know me. He said nothing, just kept on going back and forth, back and forth. He was a thin boy with pale cheeks and flat eyes. He was not a friendly person.

"I live next door," I said. "Can I ride your bike?"

He speeded up nervously, riding faster and faster, always stopping just short of the street.

"Don't you get bored doing that?" I asked. "Can I try? Give us a try. I only want to ride to the corner and back."

The boy hit the brakes and almost toppled over the handlebars in his excitement and rage at what I'd said.

"Corner! Corner!" he hollered, getting red in the face. "I'm not allowed out of the yard on this thing. Not until I've mastered this contraption."

That's what he said: "mastered this contraption." Well, that should've warned me. But I hung around, sat on the grass, waiting for him to get tired. It took a while. At last, he got off his bike, wheeled it into the garage and laid it on its side and went in the back door. All this without a word.

Seizing oppportunity, I went to the door and knocked. A lady in white pants and a bright-pink top answered.

"Can I ride the bike?" I said. The lady's mouth and eyes made O's of surprise.

"Well, I never," she said. I stood there and she stood there, neither of us giving any ground. Finally, with a litle shrug, she stood aside in a somewhat grudging way and I skinned past her. Their kitchen was like ours, only neater. There weren't dirty dishes hanging around, and the floor was shiny. The lady shook my hand without taking off her bright-pink rubber gloves. A couple of bright-pink rollers wobbled on her forehead, and I couldn't help noticing her toes. They were long toes, so long they hung over the ends of her sandals. Her toenails were painted the same bright pink as the other stuff.

The boy was nowhere in sight. Once I heard someone burp loudly out in the hall. The lady put her hand to her mouth daintily, but it wasn't her who'd burped. It was him. I'd bet on it.

"We're the Rowes," she said. "What's your name?"

"My name is Grace Schmitt," I told her. "My father's name is Frank. My mother's name is Mrs. Schmitt." I didn't want to tell her my mother's name was Grace too. It embarrassed me, to tell the truth.

"I'm in the third grade. Perhaps you'd like to come over to our house and play cards some night."

I figured somebody had to make the first move.

The lady bustled about without answering me, scrubbing away at the counter with a damp sponge, frowning as she wiped off the woodwork and the front of the refrigerator.

"You keep a very clean kitchen," I said, wanting her to know I noticed. "Your husband must be very proud of you."

The lady turned and said, "We are not a card-playing family. We have our church work, you see. As well as our crafts and community work. Our days are filled. I'm afraid not. Would you like a saltine?"

"Sure," said I, trying to sort it all out. I'd never had a saltine, but I figured if I had one it would give me time to think of something to lure the Rowes over to our house so my parents would have some friends.

The lady passed an open box of saltines in front of my face and I took one. I saw a shadowy form wearing sneakers out in the hall, so I said, "Doesn't he want one too?"

The lady let out a tinkly little laugh. "Oh, we never eat between meals. What does your father do, little girl?"

"My name's Grace," I said again, thinking she must not have heard me the first time. "He does lots of things. He's a croupier in Atlantic City, for one. Once he saw a man lose ten thousand dollars on one roll of the dice." I loved to tell that story. It always got a reaction. Today was no exception. I watched the lady's eyebrows rise until they almost collided with the rollers bobbing on her forehead. "Right at the moment," I went on, "my father's helping out at the body shop downtown. He's a very good body man," I said proudly. "One of the best."

At that moment, the boy came bounding into the room before I had a chance to tell about my mother waxing unwanted hair off people.

"Are you a Republican?" he shouted. From the way he was frowning and the way his fists were clenched, I knew he was looking for a fight.

"Sure," I said, not knowing what a Republican was, but as I was on a friend-finding mission I might as well give him answers he obviously wanted.

"It's a good thing," he said in an ominous way. "Do you get A's on your report card?" he shot at me.

I was willing to go just so far with the truth. I did have standards, after all.

"No," I said, feeling virtuous. "Sometimes I get B's."

"Mommy, tell her," the boy commanded.

The lady reached out one of her rubber gloves and smoothed the boy's hair. "Bobby never gets less than an A," she said with a trembly mouth. "He's our little scholar, aren't you, Bobby dear?"

"Okay, so hand over the five bucks," Bobby ordered.

Much to my amazement, the lady went to her purse and took out a five-dollar bill. "A reward for work well done," she cooed, placing the money in his palm tenderly, as if it'd been made of rare old china.

"They pay me a fiver every time I get all A's on my

report card," he told me, suddenly tough and with a sappy smirk on his face. "How much do you get?"

I mumbled something and said I had to go. The lady held open the kitchen door for me and didn't say, "Come again." Which was all right with me because I wouldn't even if she had.

Later that night I told my mother and father I'd invited the people next door to come over. "They don't play cards. Their lives are full," I said. "They go to church and do crafts and community work. What's a Republican?"

"The lowest of the low," said my father.

"What are we?"

"Democrats," he replied, his voice oiled with pride.

My mother turned on the TV and said, "I'll be glad when this election is over. I'm sick to death of the whole thing, and it's barely begun. All those speeches, all those promises. Hot air, that's all it is, just nothing but hot air. All that money they spend to get themselves elected. With all the poverty there is around us, it's a terrible thing. A disgrace."

Two days later I saw the boy riding his bicycle back and forth in the driveway again. I went over and said, "We're not Republicans, we're Democrats. Republicans are the lowest of the low."

He got off his bicycle, came over and punched me in the nose. It began to bleed profusely, and as intense as my pain was, my rage was more so. He took off for his house with me in hot pursuit. He'd had a head start, though, so he got inside before I caught up, and slammed the door in my face. I pounded on the door and rattled the doorknob and pushed against it, seeking revenge. But he'd already locked the door. I kept pounding and shouting. I could see them both standing there in the middle of their kitchen floor, listening, watching, waiting to see what I'd do. The lady had her arm protectively around the boy. I think I saw the five-dollar bill clutched in his hand, but I couldn't be sure.

The only thing I was sure of was that we'd never be friends. They didn't want to be friends with us because we weren't Republicans. And I didn't want to be friends with them for anything.

Even if they asked us over, I wouldn't go.

14

Buster loves to dance. I folded back the orange rug carefully and tucked it in a corner. It's Doris's pride and joy, and has to be handled with care. Then I fiddled with the radio, and when I found some nice slow music, I picked up Buster and we started out. We swooped around as if we were in a ballroom with waiters carrying trays of drinks, and women in diamond earrings and sequined gowns dancing with tall, handsome men wearing black silk suits and shirts with pleated fronts.

I don't know how to dance, as I said; but with Buster, it comes naturally. I lead, of course. He never steps on my feet, either.

"You're some snazzy dancer, kid," I told him. "Light as a feather, too." As we twirled around, faster and faster, he gave out little shouts of joy and pleasure. When I began to get dizzy, I stopped twirling, figuring if I was dizzy, he was too, and might barf all over me. Which he's been known to do.

Dancing is good for the figure, I've heard. All I know is, it's strenuous. I collapsed in a chair, breathing hard, holding on to Buster, who didn't seem winded at all. Maybe because I'd done all the work.

"Almost time for bed," I whispered, breathing into his soft little neck. He patted my cheek. He loves me. He thinks I'm beautiful. Babies are a good judge of people. Buster sees me as I really am. Every time he hugs me or laughs when I gum his little ears, he's telling me he loves me. Buster doesn't care if I wear a 38D bra. If I'm fat and ugly. He sees beyond all that.

The wind was rising, slamming against the trailer, wanting in. I hate it when the wind gets going. I put Buster in his high chair and got out his measuring spoons to keep him busy while I warmed his bottle. Doris says I don't have to bother to heat it, but I do anyway.

A couple of strong gusts of wind made the trailer sway. It must be like crossing the ocean in a storm, I thought. Lucky thing I don't get seasick. The worst thing about the wind is that it makes the trailer creak. Sometimes it sounds like a lot of people tiptoeing around. It's sort of creepy, all that creaking. I never told Doris how I felt, though. I don't like to be the scary type.

Buster just banged away on his tray with those measuring spoons. They're his favorite toy. Maybe I'll let him stay up later tonight, I thought. What difference would it make? He didn't have to get up in the morning. Besides, if he stayed up later, he'd sleep later.

I decided to make some cocoa. Sometimes Doris has marshmallows. I couldn't find any. She must've eaten them all. Doris pigs out a lot. When she's feeling blue and misses Kenny a lot, she pigs out on anything that's handy, she told me. It makes her feel better, but not for long. Lucky for Doris, she has the kind of metabolism that keeps her from ever gaining a pound. I would kill for a metabolism like Doris's.

The bottle was just about right. I tested the milk on the inside of my wrist, the way you're supposed to. I could probably get a job as a nanny if I wanted. The city paper we sometimes get on Sundays always has ads for nannies with driver's license and experience. And recent references. Lovely family with two children. Nonsmoker. Nobody, it seemed, wanted a smoker to look after their lovely family. Not that I blame them. Doris had a thing about smoking. The trailer was dotted with No Smoking signs. She didn't even bother with Please. Just No Smoking. Signs in her kitchen, her living room and in the bathroom, right over the toilet. She wasn't having Buster inhale any stale smoke into his little lungs.

Doris would give me a recent reference that'd knock your socks off. That I knew. She thought I was a first-class baby-sitter. Or I could be an au pair. Au pair means equal. An au pair lives with the family and is treated like a family member. I wouldn't mind that. But I doubt if anyone would hire me. On account of my appearance, mostly my shape. They always want someone neat and trim and attractive.

"Okay, time for eats." I took Buster out of his high chair and sat on the couch with him. It was time for my favorite TV program. Two career girls have their own apartment, and one has a boyfriend who puts the moves on the other girl when the girl who's his girlfriend is out. It's fairly hilarious. If only they wouldn't play that canned laughter. I can't stand it. It's so phony.

When Buster really gets into his bottle, his eyes almost close and he rubs his forehead with his fist, as if he's thinking big, deep thoughts. It's the cutest thing, the way he does that.

Outside, something crashed against the house. I jumped and almost cried out in alarm, but caught myself in time. Buster's eyes flew open, and he let go of the nipple and started howling.

"It's all right, darling," I said soothingly. "It's only the wind. Here you go." And I put the bottle back into his mouth, and he settled down again. It must've been the garbage cans blowing around.

I checked the clock. Ten after eight. It felt later. Rain and wind meant there'd be a sea of mud tomorrow. Kenny and Doris kept saying they were going to plant grass seed so they'd have a lawn come spring, but they never got around to it. Doris had put down some planks to make a path up to the door that visitors could walk on without dragging mud in all over her orange carpet. She was making the last payment on that carpet next month, and it would be terrible if it was ruined before it was paid for.

On the TV screen, the girl who didn't have a boyfriend was answering the door in her underwear to the boyfriend of the other girl. Those girls were always running around in their underwear, it seemed. Well, I suppose if I looked the way they did, I'd run around in my underwear too.

I got a sudden mental picture of me running around in my underwear, opening the door and finding somebody's boyfriend standing there, and I had to laugh. I mean, sometimes laughter is the only thing that keeps you sane.

Buster pushed his bottle away. He'd had enough. He always lets you know right off. I put him on my shoulder and rubbed his back. He's perfectly able to burp without me burping him, but to tell the truth, I like the closeness of him on my shoulder, the smell of him against me. So I burp him whether he needs it or not.

After a while, he let out a burp so loud it startled him. He looked up into my face as if to say, "Did *you* do that?" He looked so comical I had to laugh.

"You're a character, Buster Brown," I told him. Over the top of his head I watched the two girls sitting at the kitchen table in their underwear while the boyfriend cooked supper. Or maybe it was breakfast. Anyway, he wore a big white apron and a chef's hat, and he looked like a nerd.

Over the canned laughter, I heard a noise. Outside. Nothing much, nothing to get excited about. Sometimes raccoons got into the garbage. I turned off the sound and listened. It was only the wind and the rain battering the trailer. Maybe the wind would grab us up and whiz us to some magical place, like Dorothy in *The Wizard of Oz*. I wouldn't mind, but Doris might if she came back and found us and the trailer gone.

I settled back to watch the rest of the show, leaving the sound off. Sometimes it's fun to watch TV without sound. That way you can make up your own dialogue.

But there *was* a noise. Not raccoons, something else, something human. I was halfway up in a crouch, holding Buster to me, when I saw the door move. I know I locked it. I watched it move again. I felt my blood evaporate, my bones go cold. There was only me and Buster. Not even a dog. I reached the TV and turned up the sound very loud. I don't know why I did that—maybe to make it seem as if the room was full of people. A party was in progress.

I saw a foot wedged in the door's crack. A leg followed. If I screamed, who would hear? A person stood there. I didn't know if it was a man or a woman. The person wore a long, dark raincoat, almost touching the floor, with wide, wet shoulders and no belt. Dripping all over Doris's rug. The collar was turned up, so I couldn't see any face.

A sudden gust of wind pushed against the door, pushed the person farther into the room.

Buster pointed at the raincoat and said, "Man." Clear as anything.

The person lifted a long, wet arm and flung back the upturned collar.

I held Buster so tightly he cried out.

"Well." The raincoat's arm shoved against the door, closing it with a bang that made me jump.

"Hello, Miss Pretty," a voice said.

It was me he meant. He was talking to me.

15

My father wanted a boy. In the worst way, my mother said.

"Then there you were, a little scrap of a baby with a big, pushed-in nose, and blue lips and bowlegged. Lord, you were the most bowlegged baby I ever laid eyes on. And he took one look at you and just turned his head away. You've no idea, Grace, what that did to me. A woman has a right to expect some appreciation, some praise, wouldn't you say. After giving birth. Some sign she's done a good job."

I'd heard it all before. The good times and the bad. My parents' wedding picture showed them staring dead straight into the camera, arms entwined, eyes glossy with pride at being man and wife.

"He had such a merry heart, Grace," my mother always sighed, remembering. "Now it's gone, all gone."

I felt responsible. If I'd been a boy, maybe it wouldn't be all gone. Maybe my father's heart would still be merry. Once he told me he always wanted to be a clown. Even when he was a little boy, he said he wanted to make people laugh. Wanted to dress up in baggy pants and enormous, turned-up shoes and paint his face in a wild and extravagant way, bright reds and yellows and greens, then jump out of little cars with his shoes flapping, waving his arms and putting his face up close to the faces of the children who'd come to watch him be funny.

But like so many things, it hadn't worked out. My father had come to my mother's hometown and landed a job at Herrick's Men's Store. Formerly Herrick's Haberdashery. My mother said he was a proper dandy in those days, with the girls after him in droves.

"Oh my, yes, Mr. Herrick's business picked up considerably after your father went to work there," she told me. "Mr. Herrick thought Father's Day was here to stay. There wasn't a father or an uncle or a brother who didn't need new shirts, ties, socks, and all the girls came to buy. Your father was the hit of the town.

"Of course, in those days he had rosy cheeks and a sweet little mustache, and he wore a tattersall vest with his grandfather's gold watch chain across his chest. He was a proper dude then, all right. Had to shave twice a day, too, so his whiskers wouldn't bruise a lady's cheek."

This was my mother talking. I was afraid to breathe,

afraid any disturbance, however small, might turn her off in mid-sentence. I wanted to hear the unbelievable circumstances of my father's youth.

"Did his whiskers ever bruise your cheek?" I had to ask, thinking this a most romantic notion. She laughed and said, "Use your imagination."

I didn't need to be told to do that; my imagination had been working overtime for some years. My imagination, set into action, left almost no stone unturned. I didn't even have to close my eyes to imagine myself a princess, living in an enchanted castle, wearing sparkly red shoes and a white satin gown.

Or a movie star with a flawless complexion and a turned-up nose whose specialty was tap dancing and love scenes. I hate those love scenes where they open their mouths and slobber all over each other. That's not my idea of kissing. I think a kiss should be a tender, gentle thing. I'm not talking sex here, I'm talking kissing. They're not necessarily the same thing. Although I know one sometimes leads to another. But not always. Just because you kiss someone doesn't mean you have to leap into bed with him.

I read in the paper about a survey somebody took asking kids about their attitudes toward sex and stuff. The survey reported fifty percent of the boys surveyed wanted their wives to be virgins. And forty percent of the same group of boys said they'd already had sex. That's cutting it kind of close, I figure. Where are all those virgins supposed to come from anyway?

Nobody's ever surveyed me about anything. The Nielsen report, which keeps tabs on who watches what TV programs, has never called me to find out what I'm watching. Plenty of times I've been ready for them to call, sitting there by the telephone with my answer ready. I don't know who those Nielsen bozos call. But not me, that's for sure.

And nobody has ever surveyed me in regard to sexual practices. Half the time I think those answers are phonies, that the kids who answer the questions live in a dream world and make up the sex stuff because they're afraid to tell the truth, which is far less interesting than the lies they make up. What do I know? Probably those surveyors take one look at me and figure I'm not the kind of person who *has* any sexual practices. Probably they survey Ashley and those pals of hers at the drop of a hat. Probably Ashley's had sex since she was in sixth grade. I wouldn't put it past her.

It's none of my business what Ashley does. I try to shove her out of my thoughts. What do I care what she does? Or thinks. But she's always there. It kills me that I can't get rid of her. I dreamed of her last night. In my dream, Ashley and I were walking down the street, talking, laughing, arm in arm. We were friends. Then all of a sudden, Ashley began tearing at my clothes, ripping them off me. I put my arms around myself, trying to shield myself, but when Ashley was through and I stood there, out in the open, shivering, naked, unable to move, to speak, Ashley's friends gathered around, laughing,

pointing at me. I can't describe the feeling. Out of nowhere, then, Ms. Govoni showed up and she wrapped
a big blanket around me.

When I woke up, my face was wet. I don't remember
crying, but my face was definitely wet. It was very real,
that dream. Most dreams I forget soon after they've
happened. I wish I could forget this one. But it won't
go away. I wish I could hurt Ashley the way she's hurt
me.

If someone ever does kiss me, I hope it will be gentle
and full of meaning.

I figure as long as I look the way I do, I'm safe.

16

"That yours?" He pointed at Buster, who was drooling all over my shirt.

"No," I said, still in a state of shock at seeing him there, at what he'd said, what he'd called me. "I'm the baby-sitter."

He stayed put by the door. "Can I use the phone?" he said. "My car's broken down out on the highway." From where I was, across the room, his eyes looked black. "You got someplace I can hang this where it'll drip dry? It's soaked. Really blowing out there."

"I guess you can hang it in the bathroom so it won't get the rug all wet," I said. "Doris is very particular about her rug. It's brand-new." I got a hanger and handed it to him. Up close I could see it wasn't actually a raincoat, it was more of a tarp, the kind you put over a car in bad weather if you don't have a garage.

He took some time spreading the tarp on the hanger, fixing it so it wouldn't slip off. I could see a big damp spot on Doris's orange shag carpet, and hoped and prayed it'd be dry before she got home.

"Just stick it on the shower rod in the bathroom," I told him. He couldn't get lost looking for the bathroom. It was a small trailer and had only one bathroom.

I stood waiting, fidgeting, wishing he'd hurry up. Buster kept looking over my shoulder, keeping the guy in his sights, watching out for me. Buster is a nosy little person, in more ways than one.

When he finally came out of the bathroom, I saw his boots were covered with mud.

"Thought maybe I'd call around to see if I can get hold of a cab to take me to the nearest gas station. Maybe they've got a mechanic on duty who can fix me up." He smiled at me, rubbing his hands as if to warm them. "What do you think? Know of any good mechanics around these parts?" He put his hands in his pockets and jingled his change. It made quite a racket.

"No," I said, realizing with a mortified start that Buster had done a load in his pants. He sneaks them in, I swear he does. It seemed I only just changed him. He waits until he's got clean diapers, then he lets fly. He smelled like a baby gorilla. I pretended not to notice.

"It's okay if I use the phone then?" he said.

It hit me then, so hard I stepped backward. This had

114

to be the guy who did the number on the gas station. I tried not to look directly at him, tried to avoid eye contact, the way the experts tell you to do if some weirdo tries to hassle you.

"As long as it's not a toll call," I said, proud of the way I managed to keep my voice cool and calm. Inside, I was trembling, trying to think of what I'd do if he attacked me. Or Buster. "I guess Doris wouldn't mind." I held Buster a little bit out from me, he smelled so bad. He doesn't like to be held that way, so all of a sudden, he stiffened and threw back his head and started howling, having a temper tantrum.

"Oh, no more mister nice guy, eh?" I said.

Whenever Buster does a load in his pants, he acts like it's my fault. Ordinarily he has a very sweet disposition. It's only that one thing that gets him going.

"I doubt if anyone would come out here tonight, though," I said. "It's pretty late. Then too, the weather's not great."

He made no attempt to get closer to me, to touch me. I tried to remember what the radio announcer had said. A white male with black hair. That much I recalled, and that he wore blue jeans and cowboy boots. Well, that could describe about half the male population of the entire state. He'd escaped from prison, where he was being held on suspicion of attempted assault and rape. Terrific.

Buster stirred against me and I held him tight. He was a big help, so soft and warm and friendly in my arms. He was like an ally, a friend who was on my side.

"Terrible," the stranger agreed, letting his eyes wander, checking out the trailer and everything in it. "I think it might be my carburetor. I could fix it myself if I had a flashlight. But as it is . . ." He lifted both hands in a gesture of helplessness.

"The phone book's right there," I said.

"Thanks. Mind if I smoke?"

"Oh, you can't. Doris would have a fit. See the signs?" I poked a finger at the No Smoking signs. "On account of the baby. Doris says absolutely no smoking in her house. She's not having Buster's little lungs all contaminated with smoke. She's a bug on no smoking. She says she can smell it a mile away. Says not only does it get in your hair and clothes, it makes your breath stink." I knew I was running on, but I couldn't seem to stop. He made me nervous, the way he stood there so quiet, looking at me. Nothing moved but his eyes. They were weird eyes, all moist and glittery. Beautiful, though.

"When's Doris due back?" he asked in a conversational tone.

"Tomorrow." The minute it was out, I was sorry. For one thing, he had no business here, a total stranger. For another, it was dumb of me letting him know it was just me and Buster here alone. Really dumb.

"Well, then." He grinned at me. "It's you and me and baby makes three, right?" He stepped toward me. Whoa, I thought, panicking. I grabbed Buster so tight, he hollered to let me know I was hurting him. I shouldn't have let this guy in, I thought. But I didn't let him in, he just seeped in, like fog under the door. I had to get him out. Doris would have a fit if she found out about him being here.

"I have to change the baby," I said nervously.

"Take your time," he said. I was scared he might follow me into Buster's room, but he didn't. I changed Buster as fast as I could, wiped him off good. It's a wonder to me how a sweet little baby can smell so bad.

When I got back, he was looking out the window, pulling back the curtains, peering out into the blackness.

"Still coming down," he said, dropping the curtains when he saw me standing there.

"Did you get a mechanic?" I asked. "Or a taxi?"

"Yeah. I raised one guy, said he'd send a cab, but when he asked me where I was located, I couldn't tell him. I don't even know where I'm located. How about that?" He threw back his head and laughed uproariously. I didn't think it was *that* funny.

"You're on Old Town Road about a half mile from Route 41," I told him. "It's the Browns' trailer. They all know it. I'm surprised they said yes. Usually they don't like to come out this far. Especially on a night like this." As if to prove what kind of a night it was, a sudden gust of wind pushed open the door, sending rain onto the rug. He pushed the door shut, ignoring the slight yelp I'd let out. I told myself if one more sodden stranger

117

came into this house, I was leaving. Me and Buster both.

"I can't understand it," I said. "I know I locked that door. I can't figure how you got in."

He shrugged, as if he couldn't understand either, and went over to the telephone. I thought he was going to call the man back and tell him he was at the Browns' trailer. Instead, he stood there, fingers drumming against the table, and he said, "How come you didn't holler when you saw me? Most girls would've, seeing a stranger like that. I have to hand it to you." His voice was warm and admiring. "You never lost your cool. How'd you know I was an all-right guy, not a burglar or something?"

Pleased, in spite of myself, by the note of approval in his voice, I decided to go for nonchalance. It wasn't easy.

"What's your name?" I asked. "You from around here?" There was something familiar about him, something that made me think I might've seen him somewhere. Maybe on television or something.

"Name's Dirk Delgado," he said. "Actually, I'm from Florida, just passing through, on my way to Vegas. Ever been to Vegas?"

"No," I said, not exactly sure if he meant Las Vegas or if there was a place called plain Vegas. The answer was no, in either case.

"What's *your* name?" he asked me.

I opened my mouth to say "Grace" and thought better of it.

"Monday," I said.

"Monday, huh? What kind of name's that?" He reached out and chucked Buster under the chin. Buster was sort of standoffish when he didn't know you. He sometimes went all to pieces with strangers. I could see him trying to make up his mind about this Dirk guy. After a short spell, Buster decided in favor. He made friendly noises. The guy had passed the Buster test with flying colors.

"Hey. You're some smart kid. You know I'm on your side, don't you? Better watch it, kid. You want to be careful who you make friends with." Buster wiggled with pleasure, and without asking if it was all right, Dirk Delgado plucked Buster from me and settled in on the orange couch as cozy as if he belonged there.

"Monday's your name, huh? I never knew a girl named Monday before." He looked at me over Buster's head, expectantly, wanting more.

I took my time. "Well," I said, "there's Tuesday Weld."

"Yeah?" I could see he doubted that one.

"Sure. She's a movie actress, been around for years. Then there's Saturday Smith. She's this fabulous teen model. She's only fourteen, and already she's been on sixteen magazine covers. She's sort of gorgeous."

"Oh sure. I know her. I think maybe I've seen her in a couple centerfolds."

"Saturday Smith would never appear in a centerfold!" I said, shocked. "She's too classy for that." Even before he laughed, I knew he was pulling my leg.

"Hey, look here. Look at him, will you." Buster braced himself against Dirk's chest, showing off, showing how strong he was, how he could almost walk. Then he jounced up and down, crowing in triumph.

"You're some tiger, tiger," he told Buster. Buster made a growling sound, which made both of us laugh.

"He's a nice little kid," Dirk said. "Hope he don't grow up into some smart-ass kid, like there's a lot of them in this world, don't know their ass from their elbow, don't know nothing."

Suddenly he stood up and paced angrily back and forth, still holding on to Buster, eyes flashing, wearing a path on Doris's new carpet. His boots had those slanty heels that made him look taller than he really was. "Think because they got a BMW they're king of the hill. But they're nothing but smart-ass kids. I met a lot of those in my travels, I can tell you."

If he tied a red silk handkerchief around his neck, I bet he'd pass for a gypsy chieftain, or a pirate, with his bristly mustache and his dark hair curling over his collar. He was very good-looking in an untrustworthy sort of way.

As suddenly as he'd got up, he sat down again.

"So," he said, "your name's Monday. I like it. It's different. Memorable, like." Then he grinned and said, "How long's your name been Monday, Monday?"

I felt my cheeks get hot. "What do you mean?" I said.

He put up his hand. "Nothing. Nothing at all. Just that it sort of sounds like one of those names girls give themselves when they don't like their real name. You know? You get my meaning?"

He didn't seem to expect an answer, so I didn't give him one.

Suddenly, Buster collapsed, the way he does. One minute he's full of it, the next he's had it, ready to call it quits. He's like a balloon someone sticks a pin in— poof, he's limp. I watched him snuggle down into Dirk's chest like an old dog coming home. The guy must be all right, I reasoned, if Buster likes him.

"If you want," I said, "I can make us some coffee." I'd begun to think I was wrong about this guy.

"Hey, good idea. Coffee'd go good right now."

Doris only had instant. I got down two mugs. I'm not mad about coffee, but I figured it'd be more sociable if I had some too.

"So you're the baby-sitter, huh?" He watched me, made me self-conscious. "Been doing it long?"

"Sure. I like babies. Besides, I can use the money."

"Well, now, I'd say before long you'll have a passel of your own. You engaged? Or anything?"

Buster slept, his little mouth open, mauve eyelids fluttering, foot twitching now and then like a dog dreaming about chasing a rabbit.

I drank my coffee, too embarrassed to look at him, knowing he was grinning at me.

I shook my head no. He thought I might be engaged.

"Got a boyfriend then? Or two or three?"

He said it sort of teasing, but sort of serious, too. I pleated my shirttail and wished I had something nice on. It was an old shirt of my father's, frayed and missing buttons. I never wear anything good when I'm sitting. You never know when they're going to spit up.

"You got any milk?" He stirred the coffee with his finger, still holding on to Buster.

"Only enough for him," I said.

"Okay. Only asking. How old are you, Monday? Nineteen, twenty?" He leaned toward me, eyes crackling. I smelled cigarette smoke on him.

"Seventeen," I lied. "How about you?" I was dying to know how old he was.

He studied the ceiling. "Nineteen, no, make that twenty. Almost twenty."

All of a sudden, I don't know why, he made me uncomfortable. "Here," I reached for Buster, "better let me take him. I'll put him to bed." I don't know what it was about him. He was acting really cool, like it was the most natural thing in the world for him to be sitting in Doris and Kenny's trailer like he was an old friend of the family. Rain lashed against the walls, though the wind had died down. I noticed how he cocked his head, listening for something.

"Is the taxi coming for you?" I asked.

He snapped his fingers, remembering. "Have to give it another try. Tell him where I'm located. Old Town Road, right, half mile from Route 41. The Browns' trailer, right?"

I nodded. My palms were sweating. They always do when I'm nervous. "Excuse me," I said, and put Buster

122

down in his crib for the night. Then I locked myself in the bathroom. I always lock myself in the bathroom, even when I'm alone. I looked at myself in the mirror. That was a mistake. My hair was a mess and my face bright red. Miss Pretty. How could he resist me?

When I got back, he was standing by the telephone, hand on the receiver, as if he'd just hung up. The room was quiet. He'd turned the TV off.

"Says he can't make it tonight," he told me, shaking his head. "Maybe first thing in the morning. Okay if I stay here until then, Monday? I promise I'll be good." He flashed the grin at me. I guess I was just supposed to collapse, the way Buster had, fall into his arms. Big deal. But my knees were knocking.

"If you have to, you have to," I said casually. "I sure hope Doris doesn't come home, though. She'd have a fit. She doesn't know you or anything, I mean. Kenny tells her never open the door to a stranger. Doris said she'd be back early in the morning. She's always on time. I never knew her to be late."

"Okay, okay. I'll be gone long before Doris gets here. Never fear." He jingled his change some more. The noise of it was the only sound in the room.

"You think there's anything to eat in this place?" he said. "It's been a while since I ate."

"I'll see," I said. Usually Doris's fridge is on the empty side. She tells me to help myself to anything I want. Sometimes I bring some snacks when I come here. This

123

time I forgot. Just as well. I got a couple slices of stale bread and smeared them with peanut butter, the crunchy kind.

"Thanks," he said. Without warning, he pulled me down on the couch next to him. "Hey," he said, taking a bite, "good. You make a good sandwich, all right." The hand not holding the sandwich took me by the back of the neck. "Hey," he said. Stunned, not accustomed to body contact, I sat, frozen, waiting for what would come next.

Still holding me, he took a knife from his pocket and showed it to me.

"See this little beauty?" he said, running his thumb over the blade, barely touching it. "She's my friend, she never lets me down. I take her everywhere. I can trust her. She's like a beautiful woman, you know?"

It hurt me to breathe. I licked my lips and nodded.

"Silent and deadly." He laughed, and it was a strange and joyless sound. "Get it, Monday? Beautiful woman, silent and deadly."

Goose bumps crowded on my spine. He laid the knife on his knee and took my other hand in his.

"Know what, Monday? I can read your life line," he said. "I can tell you in one look how long you got to live." He blew on my palm and scrubbed it with his hand as if cleaning it off.

"What's this? This thing here." With a finger he traced the V William had cut into my skin so long ago. "What's this, where'd this come from?" he asked.

124

"When I was really little, this boy and I were going to be blood brothers." I stopped, trying to steady my voice. He kept up the tracing until I thought I would scream, it tickled so bad.

"So we sucked each other's blood to make us blood brothers." I could see it as if it were yesterday. "William cut his hand too, only not so much as mine, and the blood wouldn't stop so we had to go to the hospital. That's about it."

I closed my eyes and put my head against the back of the couch. He's going to hurt us, I thought in despair. I don't care about me. . . . What a lot of bull! Of course I cared about me. But if he let Buster alone, I'd try not to mind too much about me.

If only I could get the knife away from him, I thought, maybe I could do something—fight him off, call the police. Anything.

As if from a great distance, I heard him say, "What happened to the kid who cut you?"

Keeping my eyes closed, I said I didn't know. "At the end of the summer, we went back home and I never saw him again. He went to Florida with his mother and her boyfriend."

He was quiet for a while. I could hear him breathing. Then he asked, "What did you say his name was, the kid who cut you?"

"William," I said, seeing William and myself on the boardwalk, running. We spent that whole summer running, it seemed. "He was my first best friend. We had such a good time. I'll never forget it. He almost drowned, and an old man pulled him out of the waves and we didn't tell anybody."

I felt his breath on my face. My eyes snapped open. His face was very close to mine, his eyes glittering at me. I felt drawn into them, almost as if a magnet was hidden in their strange depths.

He took his hand away from my neck then and said, "Better get some shut-eye, Monday. That little baby's going to be up with the birds. I'll take off first light, see if I can get on the road real early."

Like an old lady with arthritis, I got up. "Sure," I said. The knife lay there. He picked it up and put it in his pocket.

Buster was lying with his little butt pointed at the ceiling. I would've locked the bedroom door, but there wasn't any lock on it. I considered dragging the bureau over so it'd block the door, in case he tried to get in, and decided against it. Don't be a total ass, I told myself. I pulled the quilt over myself without undressing. Arms and legs as heavy as lead, I melted into the mattress.

I was exhausted, but I couldn't sleep. I imagined him out there, pacing, peering out the window, waiting for the storm to subside. Probably I shouldn't have gone to bed, should've waited up with him.

Maybe he was okay. Maybe my imagination was going haywire.

Then a shadow moved. The room was pitch-black, but I swear I saw a shadow standing by the bed. If I sat up and said, "Who's there?" he'd kill me. I was certain of that. If I pretended to be asleep, he might let me alone.

I smelled him. He was there, beside me. On the bed.

Oh God, I thought, help me.

Then I felt his face, his mouth on mine. He kissed me. Not hard, not passionately, just kissed me gently, with love and kindness.

I was stunned.

The shadow moved and was gone. I waited, planning what I'd say if he spoke.

I knew he was gone. I knew the room was empty of everyone but me and Buster. I turned on my side and slept without dreaming.

17

I was the kind of person who was never sure when to laugh. For the longest time, whenever something funny happened, I held back until the last minute, until I was sure it was all right, until everyone else had finished laughing, then I'd laugh. Sometimes I laughed so long and so hard people looked at me strangely, as if to say, "What's with *her?*" or "Who's the crazy?"

And for the longest time, I couldn't tell time. If there was a digital clock or watch handy, I could read off the numbers. But when it came down to telling time by a wristwatch or an ordinary clock, I was lost. I tried to fake it, but people always caught on. I think I was in the eighth grade before I finally got it down, and even then I hesitated, the same way I hesitated when it came to laughing, before I said firmly, "It's ten to eight," or, "Twenty-three to six." Or, "Thirty-one past three." I wanted to be exact, wanted everyone to know I had the matter under control.

Once in a while I have a dream in which I'm in a room full of people. They're all looking at me and asking me to tell them the correct time. I call off the answers in a strong, loud, sure voice. But they don't stop shooting questions at me. No matter how many times I answer correctly, they keep it up.

I don't know why it took me so long. I tied my own shoes early, learned to dress myself, even get my arms in the right sleeves, my shoes on the right feet. I could button buttons, and I was toilet trained before I was two. But the thing people always remembered was that I couldn't tell time. It's funny how that happens. No matter how many things you're good at when you're little, they always remember the thing you couldn't do.

That might not sound like much, but it was. Is.

My father had his gall bladder out when I was nine. I can remember going to the hospital with my mother to visit him. He was in a ward with eight or ten other men. The beds were lined up neatly, the men tucked into them, so flat that all that disturbed the neatness was the men's feet sticking up, making little mounds at the foot of the bed. My father had on his pajamas printed all over with little sailboats, and his fuzzy blue bathrobe lay on his bed. His slippers were on the floor where he could get at them easily.

"Well, how are you?" we said. My mother had brought him a plant that I'd helped pick out. We stood around holding it until she finally put it on the windowsill. She asked him about the food, if the doctor had been in to see him that day, what he'd said. How was he getting on, when would he be able to come home.

Everything was fine and dandy, my father told us. His bones looked as if they were about to poke right through his skin. I felt very shy among all those sick people. There was a funny smell in that room that I didn't care for, and when I wrinkled my nose and, once, held it closed with my fingers, my mother frowned at me and made me take my hand away from my face. The nurse came down the aisle between the beds. Her thick-soled white shoes made squeegee noises on the tile floor, and her glasses glinted in the pale sun, which fought its way through the murky windows. She stuck a thermometer into my father's mouth, and we all stood there quietly until she took it out, looked at it and wrote something on the chart at the foot of my father's bed.

An old man lying in the next bed seemed to be alseep. But when I looked over at him, his eyes were open. They were like a bird's eyes, very small and quick.

"Those your sisters?" he asked my father in a squeaky voice. My father said no, we were his wife and daughter. "This is my wife, Grace," my father said, "and my daughter, Grace. Mr. Timmons."

"Which one is Grace?" the old man said, and my father laughed. My mother and I didn't. I knew from my mother's face she didn't think it was funny. I wasn't sure what I thought.

"I had a wife once." The old man raised himself on one elbow. "She had two left feet and she kept salt in her belly button."

I looked over at my mother, wondering if I should laugh now. But her face remained stony, and she pretended she hadn't heard what the old man had said.

"You want to know why she kept salt in her belly button?" the old man asked me. His little eyes were looking straight at me. My father said, "It's all right, Grace."

"Why?" I said.

"Why," said the old man, "she liked to eat celery in bed. Now you can't very well eat celery without salt, can you? That's why she kept a supply in her belly button." Then he lay back down, closed his eyes and said no more.

I wanted to laugh. I felt a great swell of laughter rising in my stomach. But my mother looked so severe and my father so unwell, I didn't dare. I swallowed my laughter in great gulps, hoping it wouldn't cause gas later on and give me a stomachache. At that point in my life, I was famous for stomachaches. My mother went around with a bottle of Milk of Magnesia, like a mother in a TV commercial.

On the bus going back home my mother maintained a disapproving silence. She sat next to the window; she always sat next to the window. I would've liked to sit there now and then but she never asked me, she just slid in first. She got to see the sights, and I got to look at the back of the bus driver's head.

"I thought that was a funny story," I said as we approached our stop. My mother turned her head slowly, as if she had a stiff neck and it hurt her to make any movement.

"I only hope I don't live that long," she said in a cold voice. "When senility sets in, it's hard on everyone. Especially the loved ones. The poor old man's wife. Imagine him telling a story like that about her." She clicked her tongue, making a *tch tch* sound, and pushed me ahead of her down the aisle, fearful that we might not get off in time, that the bus door would slide shut and we'd be trapped forever more.

When my father came home from the hospital, he looked worse than when we'd gone to see him. My mother was working then, so she told me to be sure to come straight home from school (as if I ever did any different) and make sure my father was all right.

We played go fish and he always let me win. When he got up to go to the bathroom, I could see it hurt him to walk. "Are you all right?" I asked. He always said the same thing.

"Never better, darling" was what he said. I really did want to know how he was feeling, but the main reason I asked him that was I liked it when he called me "darling."

Every afternoon I made my father cinnamon toast and

132

tea, and carried it to him on a tray. I set a little plastic flower in a glass of water, and put it on the tray to decorate it and make it seem more festive.

"My, my," my father always said, as if surprised, pulling himself upright in bed. I put a second pillow behind him and drew up a chair. Sometimes, when he was feeling up to it, I read him parts of my diary.

"To what do I owe all this fanciness?" he liked to ask me. He sipped at his tea and ate a little toast, though not with much enthusiasm. I ate the rest.

"I enjoyed meeting your friend Mr. Timmons," I said in what I considered a ladylike way. "Does he have to stay in the hospital a long time?"

"Well," said my father, "I think he's on his way out."

"You mean he's going home soon, same as you?" I asked, nibbling daintily on a cinnamon crust.

"No." My father's long Schmitt face seemed very sad. "I mean he's on his way out. Of this world. He doesn't have long to live is what I mean. His wife died six months ago, and the nurse told me the old boy sort of gave up. Just as well. He doesn't have anyone left. No one to take care of him. He's not lucky like me." He patted my hand, and I took the tray back to the kitchen. I didn't want my father to see how his news had upset me.

Poor little Mr. Timmons. I felt so bad I hadn't laughed, the way I wanted to, at his belly-button story. Wished I'd had the courage to laugh out loud instead of holding in my laughter until it was too late.

133

18

I woke with a sense of apprehension. What if he was still there, waiting? Knife in hand, running his thumb over the blade, watching me with those strange eyes.

I listened.

Buster was giving his teddy-bear mobile a workout. My mouth felt gummy, my eyelids brittle and frail, as if they might break off. I ran my hand over my face, to see if there were any traces of his lips. Any indentation. Or burn marks. Nothing.

I sat up, wondering if it had really happened or if it was a figment of my imagination. Maybe I had hallucinated and he hadn't kissed me at all. I got up and stumbled into the bathroom, first checking the living room, although I knew it'd be empty. I felt sticky and unclean.

The tarp was gone from the shower rod.

I avoided looking in the mirror while I brushed my teeth. No amount of brushing helped. My mouth still felt gummy.

Buster was still giving his bears a workout. I checked the living room for cigarette butts. Maybe he'd smoked after I went to sleep. The room was clean. It didn't smell of smoke. Thank God. Doris had a nose like a bird dog when it came to sniffing out cigarette smoke. I even got down and checked under the couch and chair for anything telltale there.

There was no sign of his having been there. He had skinned out without leaving a trace.

Buster greeted Doris with "Ma ma ma" when she got home. Then he went into "Man man man."

"Will you listen to him!" Doris was beside herself. "Is he some smart kid!"

When Doris dropped me off, she gave me a hug and a dollar tip, and said, "What would we do without you, Gracie? You're the best." I love Doris. She always makes me feel good about myself, leaves me with a kind of glow—which unfortunately never lasts long.

I felt as if I'd been away a week. My father seemed to have got older in my absence. He looked as if he'd shrunk, although maybe it was just the huge white apron he wore. He was peeling potatoes and watching a game show.

"There you are, Grace. Tried to call you last night to see how you were doing with the storm and all. Lines

135

were down, they said. You make out all right?" He wielded his potato peeler like a pro.

Funny. Dirk said he'd called a taxi from the trailer, as well as a mechanic.

"It was okay." I went to my room and lifted my hair and backed up to the mirror to see if there were burn marks on the back of my neck. Where his hand had been. I couldn't see anything, but the skin felt scorched.

"Grace, I've got soup going. Have a bowl, it'll warm you up." My father said that even when the temperature was in the eighties. He had the knack of tossing old bones, old gravy and old veggies into a pot and turning them into delicious soup.

I wondered how tall Dirk would be without the slanty-heel cowboy boots. Not much taller than me, I bet.

Doris had nuzzled Buster and asked, "Anything happen while I was gone?" I mumbled, "Same old stuff," and changed the subject. Some things were better left unsaid.

"Two more announced they're running for the presidency," my father said. "Why anyone wants that job is beyond me." He shook his head. "And they're still looking for that fella shot the gas-station man," my father said, blowing on his soup discreetly, cooling it. "A thousand bucks goes for information leading to his arrest. Nice piece of change, that. Not bad. Wouldn't mind a thousand big ones myself. A thousand bucks," he repeated, relishing the sound and taste of it. "A nice piece of change, I call it."

136

I choked a little, and my father made me hold my arms over my head and pounded me on the back to make me stop choking. *Was* Dirk the man they were looking for?

"There he is." My father folded back the newspaper and showed me a picture of the escapee. "Looks like a nice fella now, not a cold-blooded killer. Can't judge a book by its cover, that's for sure."

I studied the face. It had a beard and a mustache that almost wiped out his mouth. It could've been him; on the other hand, it could've been some other guy. The eyes were strange, like Dirk's eyes. But the rest of him, I don't know. And didn't *want* to know. It made me feel a little sick to think about. I opened my hand and looked at my scar. That scar had interested him. I felt his finger tracing it over and over.

A thousand dollars would go a long way toward my operation, though.

He was long gone, probably out of the state by now. They'd never catch him. Even if he was the right one, the one they were looking for, what good would it do telling them what I knew, which was zilch? Except that he'd been in the trailer. His fingerprints were on the phone.

My father snapped his fingers and said, "Almost forgot, Grace. Ms. Govoni called, said she'd be here at three sharp to pick you up."

Oh Lord, I'd forgotten I said I'd baby-sit for her today. All I wanted was to be alone, to think about what had happened last night. To sort things out in my head.

137

Probably he was just some handsome, no-good weirdo passing through, on his way to Vegas, like he'd said. Only that and nothing more.

"Thanks, Dad. She's my gym teacher. She has two kids. I like her. She's been nice to me. They make fun of her at school, say nasty things about her. But she's a good, kind person."

I almost never told my father anything about school, the people in it. The ones I liked or didn't like. I really almost never talked to him, when you came down to it. He looked startled, then pleased.

"If you like her, Grace, she must be all right," he said. "You have to trust your own judgment. That's part of growing up. We won't always be here, your mother and me, I mean. To tell you what's what. Want some more?"

"No thanks," I said. "I better take a shower and change my clothes. Thanks for the soup. Nobody makes soup like yours."

What *is* what? I wondered. And when had they last told me?

Studying myself in the mirror, I decided I'd been born a couple hundred years too late. Back then, fat was in. Only they called it voluptuous. If you had big boobs and a big behind and rolls of fat around, some famous artist would most likely tell you to strip, then paint you in the nude, horsing around with a merry band of cherubs, all with rolls of fat, and you'd wind up hanging on

138

the wall of some world-renowned museum where anyone who felt like it could look at you.

If I narrowed my eyes and stared at myself in a mirror all fogged up with steam from the shower, I might pass for presentable. And surely voluptuous.

Looks aren't everything, after all.

Oh yeah? Somebody had screwed up on mine something fierce.

Sometimes the dialogue I exchange with myself beats anything I can handle in the real world, talking to real people.

Ashley, I'm going to say. Ashley, you shithead. You're the biggest, most disgusting shithead in the world. You know what should happen to you? They should shave all your hair off and strip you naked and then parade you in the streets, the way they did to French women who collaborated with the Nazis in the war. Those women were outcasts, they were despised, so the French people humiliated them and treated them like shit.

Then, they should put you in the stocks, like in Colonial days. You'd have your wrists and ankles held in those holes in the stocks, and there you'd be, shaved and naked, and the people would come and stone you. Sometimes they stone people to death. That's okay, Ashley. I'm not against that in extreme cases. In your case, stoning you to death might be called poetic justice. If there was any poetry involved. You've got it coming.

I once read a short story by Shirley Jackson called

"The Lottery." It was about a person being stoned to death. The first time I read it, I thought it was a bizarre and terrible story, sort of unreal, like a fantasy or science fiction story. Then I read it several more times, and each time it became more real in my head. It's an amazing story and also perfectly plausible. Life, I've decided, is often more terrible than anything a writer can make up.

"Grace, it's Ms. Govoni here for you."

I emptied my head of Ashley and arranged my face in what passed for happy, and went out to the kitchen.

"Then you take whatever's lying around," my father was saying, "and throw in a good handful of salt, maybe a bouquet garni, some parsley, garlic, thyme, whatever suits you, and just let it simmer awhile."

"Your father's giving me his soup recipe," Ms. Govoni told me. She looked different somehow, and it took me a while to realize she was wearing a dress.

Still in his apron, my father was oozing charm from every pore. I didn't even know he knew words like "bouquet garni."

"Grace told me all about you, Ms. Govoni," he said. "It's a pleasure meeting you." He waved us to the car and watched as we peeled off.

Discreetly, I checked Govoni's feet. She actually had on heels.

"Bet you thought I didn't own a pair of real shoes," she said, catching me at it. I laughed, and the backseat broke into giggles.

"They're hiding," she said. "They always do when there's a new sitter. They like to see what she's like. Or he. We had a wonderful boy sitter, but he's off and running on a college basketball scholarship now."

"They" came up for air. "She means Greg!" they hollered. The boy said, "If Greg was in this car right now his head would touch the roof, he's so tall." The little girl nodded. "Greg is very, very tall, and he lets us stay up very, very late, until nine o'clock sometimes." They were as alike as two peas, brown hair, brown, almond-shaped eyes.

"Rosie is six and Mack is seven." Ms. Govoni introduced us. "This is Grace Schmitt, children. Be polite and she'll love you."

"Do you like children?" A small, damp hand grazed my ear.

"Sometimes," I said. "Not always. I baby-sit a baby named Buster. He's very, very little, and sometimes we dance together and he takes bubble baths."

"He's a boy and he takes bubble baths?" asked Mack, incredulous.

"Sure. They make him sneeze."

They thought that was funny and laughed all the way home. It was a good beginning. Ms. Govoni lived in a two-family house, on the second floor. She slept on the pullout couch in the living room, and the kids had bunk beds in the bedroom. The refrigerator door was wall-to-wall crayoned drawings of people and houses and dogs.

"We're getting a dog when we get big," Rosie said.

"A dog is a big responsibility," Mack agreed.

"Supper is spaghetti, and there are plenty of greens if you want to make a salad, Grace," Ms. Govoni said. "Fruit for dessert."

"Greg always let us have Mars bars," Mack said sternly.

"Greg didn't pay the dentist bills." She kissed them good-bye. It was odd, seeing Govoni as a mother rather than a gym teacher.

"And no television until after supper, remember." She turned to me. "They'll fill you in on everything, Grace. They're better than reading the newspaper. Be good, kids, and treat Grace with lots of TLC so she'll want to come again."

When she had gone, they circled me, eyeing me, trying to get the lay of the land.

"We're adopted," Mack said. "We *were* Korean, but now we're American."

"We're *still* Korean," Rosie said. "Only now we live in America and we eat American food and our mother is American. But we're *still* Korean."

The doorbell rang, saving me from having to answer them.

"He has to be paid," Rosie said. "The paperboy. He always gets paid on Saturday. I bet she forgot to leave money."

The paperboy turned out to be Walter, aka Croc. When he saw me he took a step backward and scratched his head. "I must have the wrong place," he said.

"She's the baby-sitter," Rosie told him. "My mother forgot the money."

"She owes me for two weeks," Croc said. "That's two fifty she owes me. Don't forget. I can't carry a customer more 'n two weeks without paying. That's the rules." Croc looked out at me from under shaggy eyebrows. "You're Grace," he told me.

"No, I'm Monday." I took the paper from him and closed the door. Then I read four books to Mack and Rosie, and they, in turn, read five to me.

"Why did you tell him your name was Monday, when it's Grace?" Mack wanted to know.

"When I get bored with Grace I switch around," I said. "There's nothing that says you can't change your name if you feel like it."

The newspaper lay folded on the table. I could see half of a man's bearded face looking at me.

"What time do you eat supper?" I asked.

"Five," said Rosie.

"If we eat at four, then we can watch cartoons earlier." Mack watched for my reaction.

"True," I nodded. "But are you hungry that early?"

"Sure," they said. We settled on four thirty. I made a nice salad and had some with them while they ate spaghetti.

"Are you on a diet?" Mack asked.

"Yes," I said, although I hadn't been until now. We each had a pear for dessert.

STILL AT LARGE the headline said. The man was much

older than Dirk, I could see. His mouth was tucked in, as if he was sucking on a lemon. His dark eyes were blank and cruel. The police were still hunting him.

"He is well-spoken and devious," the story said. "Charming and self-centered and very manipulative, especially with women. He is considered very dangerous and, in addition to the robbery and shoot-out at the Amoco station, is wanted for questioning in the attempted rape and assault of two high school girls last year. The escapee, whose real name is said to be in doubt, uses several aliases, among them William Williams, William Scott, Dirk Williams and Dirk Delgado. Residents are warned to be on the lookout. All information will be held in strict confidence. Call this number."

We played slapjack and crazy eights. Mack asked if I'd like to play chess with him, and I told him I didn't know how. He said he'd teach me, that he was just learning himself, but I knew he'd beat me even so.

"How were they?" Ms. Govoni asked when she returned. "Did they give you the rundown on their genealogy? Tell you they're adopted and half Korean, half American?"

"They told me all about it," I said.

"They tell everyone," she said, laughing, taking a container of orange juice from the fridge. "Want some?" I shook my head. "Everywhere we go. The supermarket, church, the library, never mind school. They spare no detail. I'd wanted to adopt a child for some time, but

144

it's not easy, especially when you're single. Then a friend put me in touch with an agency that places Korean orphans. They showed me a picture of Rosie and Mack. They were holding hands and looking at me, and I knew they were the ones, though I'd only planned on one. That was almost four years ago. I've never been sorry."

"You must love them a lot," I said. "They're wonderful kids."

"They fill my life. I won't say I haven't had second thoughts. When one of them wakes at two A.M. with a temperature of a hundred and six degrees or falls out of a tree headfirst, I freak out. But I guess every mother freaks out now and then. And that's what I am, a mother." She shook her head. "No one is more amazed than I am."

I'd made up my mind I wouldn't tell Ms. Govoni about last night, about Dirk. She had enough to think about without getting that much more tied up with me and my problems. Besides, she was so kind, so caring, it might upset her if I said I thought he was the escaped criminal the police were looking for. When you thought about it, it really *was* scary.

So I told her about saving my baby-sitting money for a breast reduction operation. I told her about the weasely kid calling me fat mama. But all the time I was talking, I was thinking about Dirk. About how he looked, what he said. About him kissing me.

"Poor Grace," she said. "People are awful. You don't need any operation, though. I believe in staying away

145

from surgery if possible. If you lost some weight and got a really good bra, you'd be fine. Lots of people would envy you your shape. You'll see. And next time that kid calls you fat mama, do one of two things." She smiled at me. "Punch him in the nose as hard as you can. Or sidle up to him and whisper you'd like to get to know him better. Either way, I bet he runs. You've got to call his bluff."

We laughed at that. Laughing always makes me feel better, more relaxed. One of the reasons I can talk so easily to Ms. Govoni is that she has a light touch. Even when we discuss serious things, she never gets really tense. Maybe that's because I'm not her kid. I don't know the reason, but it really encourages me to confide in her.

Then, without thinking, I began to tell her about the events of last night, the very ones I'd made up my mind *not* to tell her. I *had* to tell someone. I told her about Dirk coming into the trailer, about the tarp he wore, about how Buster had liked him, about his knife. I told her about my scar and how I'd got it from William. I talked about how he'd traced the scar and asked me where it came from, and how, when I told him, he'd changed. I told her I thought he might kill me or Buster or both of us. Whatever I'd said made him change his mind about killing us, I was sure of that. When I told him about William, he let me alone. He kissed me. I told her that, too.

All the time I was talking, she listened without saying

a word. When I was finished, she laid her hand on mine and said, "Well, that's the most fascinating and awful story I've heard in a long time, Grace. And you got through it without losing your cool. Congratulations. Lots of kids, never mind grown women, would've had hysterics. You're very brave. I admire you tremendously for behaving in such a mature way, thinking of Buster instead of yourself."

I hadn't thought of myself as brave. Maybe I was! I felt proud that she thought so.

"It's hard to escape the conclusion that Dirk and William are one and the same person, isn't it?" she asked me. I nodded.

"Wouldn't that be the most bizarre coincidence?" she said. "William turning up in the person of Dirk in the Browns' trailer after all those years! It really is too much."

I kept nodding, wanting her to keep talking. She was putting my thoughts into words for me—something I'd been reluctant to do because it sounded so weird. The whole thing was weird. But that didn't mean it couldn't have happened. Like in "The Lottery."

"How about the police?" Ms. Govoni said. "Did you report it to them yet? Let them take it from there."

"If I told them, they'd think I was crazy or something," I said. "They'd think I was a kook. Maybe I'll tell them. I haven't made up my mind yet."

Then Ms. Govoni cracked a silly joke that broke both of us up. We laughed so much, Rosie and Mack came running, wanting to know what was so funny.

"Time to take Grace home, kids. It's later than I thought."

The children groaned, knowing they'd blown it. "If only you'd stayed quiet," Mack said, "they would've forgotten about us, Rosie."

They raced down the stairs ahead of us, shouting with glee. When you're little, it's easy to be happy, I thought.

We followed more sedately, Ms. Govoni and I.

"You can make something wonderful of yourself, Grace," she told me. "You have great potential. The important thing is to have faith in yourself."

"I want to kiss Grace good-bye." Rosie's wiry little arms went around my neck from the backseat. "I love you, Grace," Rosie said.

"You just met her," Mack said in a gruff voice. "You can't love somebody you just met."

"Yes I can. Can't I, Mommy?"

"Absolutely," Ms. Govoni said. "That's known as love at first sight."

Later, I lay awake, thinking about things. Dirk, Ashley, Ms. Govoni, Mack, Rosie. Love at first sight. Monday I love you.

Now if only I had faith in myself.

19

Lucy and I sat on her bed, planning her birthday party. Lucy's bedroom looked like a bedroom in a magazine—all pink and white, billowing organdy. It was a dream bedroom, and even now, if I close my eyes, I can see the two of us sitting on Lucy's white organdy spread.

"We're going to have scads of balloons," said Lucy, "and a clown."

"A live clown?" I asked, not willing to show how deeply this impressed me.

"Well, you certainly don't think we're having a dead one, do you?" Lucy's scorn was monumental and shamed me into silence.

"My mother's fixing creamed chicken in those little patty shells you get at the bakery." Lucy licked her lips and rearranged the mounds of little pillows piled on her bed. What did she do with them at night, I wondered, when she went to sleep?

"And peas, of course. And the cake's going to be chocolate with chocolate frosting and chocolate-chip ice cream."

I was stunned, never having heard of, much less gone to, such a party. The only birthday parties I knew were made up of one or two guests, pale and silent and ill at ease, children whose mothers were acquaintances, even, perhaps, customers, of my mother.

"That sounds nice," I said, barely able to contain my excitement.

"And little baskets of candy, and of course"—Lucy's eyes sought mine and I could see even she was thrilled by this tidbit—"everyone gets a favor. My mother says it's not nice for just the hostess to get presents. She says everyone should go home with a little something, just to show they've been to a party. She says when she was a girl in Memphis, they had a silver tea service on the sideboard, and whenever they gave a party, the servants polished the tea service so's you could see your face in it for weeks afterward."

As if on cue, Lucy's mother appeared in the doorway and said, "Well, darling, and who's *today's* little visitor?" as if they had a constant stream. Even before I stood up, because she was an older person and I'd been taught to stand as a mark of respect, I knew Lucy's mother had dismissed me from her thoughts. Her pale, liquid eyes took me in as Lucy said, "This is Grace Schmitt, Mother."

"Ah," sighed Lucy's mother, "Grace Schmitt. And where do you live, Grace?"

I told her, and with a narrow hand she brushed her forehead as if wiping away cobwebs. It was not an address that spoke of pink-and-white bedrooms, nor was it an address that drew anyone's approval. I had never lived at such an address and probably never would.

"Lucy, my love, it's time for the dentist."

Lucy bounced off the organdy spread, and I knew it was time for me to say good-bye.

"I'll see you," I said, and Lucy's mother straightened Lucy's collar and whispered something into her ear. I had always been taught it was impolite to whisper.

"Good-bye," I said as they got into their car. "Good-bye, Lucy, I can hardly wait," I said. They drove off, leaving me on the sidewalk. I thought I saw Lucy's hand waving to me from the car window, but I couldn't be sure.

I went home and told my mother I had to have a new dress for Lucy's party. She rummaged through the closet and brought forth one of her dresses, which she held against me and said she believed it could be cut down to fit me. Close to tears, I said no, it would never, never fit me. No matter what was done to it.

By great good fortune, next day a local store advertised in the paper a half-off sale on girls' dresses. We hurried on down, and I wound up with a nice, if uninteresting, yellow dress. Yellow wasn't my color, but what was?

My father polished my patent-leather shoes with Vaseline until they shone. I could see my face in them almost as clearly as Lucy's mother could see hers in the silver tea service on the sideboard. I took a bath every day in anticipation of Lucy's party.

My mother gave me a shampoo and a vinegar rinse and would've gladly removed any unwanted hair if I'd had any. The whole family sat back and waited for the invitation to arrive.

"It will come by mail," my mother announced. "If they're having creamed chicken and all that, they'll mail those invitations. You can be sure of that."

I saw Lucy every day at school. She didn't mention the party. But I heard her as she reeled off the details to a crowd of eager listeners. Well, after all, I told myself somewhat smugly, I'd heard them first. I knew all about the clown and the favors. As well as the chocolate-chip ice cream. I'd also been the first to sit on Lucy's white organdy spread. You can't have everything.

Days passed. Finally, unable to stand the suspense any longer, I asked Lucy what day the party was to be. What time. I was going out to buy the present that very afternoon, I told her.

"Oh," said Lucy, putting her hand to her mouth, widening her eyes in perplexity, "I'm not inviting you."

I stood very still, afraid if I moved, I'd overflow, like

152

a jug of water that's filled too full. I put out my hand and said, "But you told me I was. You said, you told me about everything. The clown. Why did you tell me? I have a new dress, even. I thought I . . ."

Lucy stamped her foot. I had made her angry. "Oh no," she said in a pitying tone. "I never said you were invited. We can only fit in ten. My cousins are coming *just* for my party. There isn't room. I did *not* say you were invited. You just thought you were."

And she spun on her heel and left me there. I could barely move, surrounded as I was by ruined pride and hopes and dreams. I don't remember the rest of that day. But I do remember how my mother and father looked when I told them it had all been a mistake. Their faces crumpled, as if they'd been made of some soft stuff that came apart at a touch.

"She has to have her cousins, you see," I announced in a feeble attempt at not caring. "They only have room for ten. Her cousins are coming all that way just for the party."

I escaped then, ran into my room and slammed shut the door.

For once, my mother didn't come tapping, asking me what was wrong.

For once, she knew.

The thing that nagged at me, after the pain had gone down a little, was: What were the favors?

I would never know.

20

I've decided two things: One, I'm not having any breast operation. Two, I'm not ratting on Dirk. I can't. He might be William, my first real friend. I'll probably never know for sure. It's better that way. I'd hate to think William had turned to a life of crime. And if it really was Dirk and he had spared my life for some unknown reason, I can imagine him the way he was when he kissed me. It's very complicated. I still don't have it sorted out in my head. Maybe I never will.

I played hooky on and off after everything had happened. I felt too frail for any kind of encounter with anyone. I was tempted to play sick, stay in bed, but I knew if I did, I might never get up.

It turned out all right. I acted as normal as I could. Nobody said anything to me. I saw Ashley from a distance. She steered clear of me.

It's got so I sit for Rosie and Mack every Saturday. Four straight Saturdays now I've sat for them. We do exercises on the living-room rug. Ms. Govoni believes you're never too young to keep the bod in shape. She has them, and me, doing sit-ups, stretch exercises, leg lifts—all that kind of stuff. At first I was self-conscious in front of the kids, but they acted as if it was the most ordinary thing in the world for the three of us to be out flat on the floor, so now it's fun.

Ms. Govoni's taking a psychology course at the community college. She plans on getting a degree in child psychology. "Children need help," she told me, "and I'd like to be able to give it to them." She doesn't want to be a gym teacher all her life, she said. "I'll probably have to take out a bank loan to see me through. I don't like to borrow money, but if I do, I want to be sure it's for a good reason. I guess education's as good a reason as any."

It's also got so that when Walter (Croc) comes to deliver the paper every Saturday, he winds up hanging around for a while, shooting the breeze with me and the kids, even peering into the refrigerator now and then to see what's what. He never takes anything though. He knows better.

When I pay him the money Ms. Govoni leaves, it's

155

amazing the way he just eases himself into a sitting position while still standing, bends his knees just so and backs up to the couch gradually until, next thing I know, he's sitting there, smiling around the room, the uninvited and expectant guest. I can't remember ever asking him to sit, but there he is, settling in for a good chat.

"You ever try octopus?" he asks, letting his ropey old hands hang down between his knees, studying them like there's a message written on them.

"No," I tell him, thinking that's a funny way to start a conversation, "I never did."

Rosie and Mack, who are never far away, come bounding out from wherever they're hiding, shouting, "Oh yes, oh yes, octopus is very delicious!" Then Rosie rubs her stomach and proclaims, "Octopus is very yummy and tasty," as if she's heard it described on TV that way. As if octopus is a cereal with sugar coating.

Walter pauses, scowling, tapping a long finger against the side of his head.

"How about raw hamburger?" he says slyly.

"Raw hamburger! Whoever heard of eating raw hamburger?" the kids cry, jumping around like fleas on a stray dog. He waits until they calm down before he opens his eyes wide and says, "With a raw egg on top?"

Well, that gets them. They zoom around, hands clapped over their mouths to hold back possible vomiting. They love it, they love Walter. Ms. Govoni says they spend time during the week thinking up weird foods to pull on him. When he shows up, they shout, "Cauliflower!" which they find outrageous. Or "Brussels sprouts!" which I find outrageous, and he makes a big deal out of being astonished, rolling his eyes and clutching himself by the throat, making gagging sounds, which sends them off into more gales of laughter.

I made the mistake of telling Estelle about Walter being Ms. Govoni's paperboy, and the end of her nose started to twitch.

"He's a complete dinosaur," she said. "A positive troglodyte." All of a sudden, Estelle's into natural history and conservation. She's also thinking of taking Latin or Greek next year if she can find any around. Ever since she totaled her mother's car, Estelle's a different person. She never misses a Sunday at church, for instance, and she's also into culture. Instead of listening to Tina Turner or Billy Joel, now she tunes in to Luciano Pavarotti. It's amazing what a brush with the grim reaper can do.

At first, Estelle's mother was so overjoyed that Estelle didn't have so much as a scratch on her, she kept hugging and kissing her and thanking God he'd spared her baby. Then, after a few days, the euphoria wore off and Estelle's mother got so mad about her totaled car, which she hadn't even finished paying for, that Estelle said her life wasn't worth a plugged nickel and she was thinking about leaving home. She asked if she could come and live with us, but my mother said one teenager was enough. For once, I agreed with my mother. When I tried to imagine Estelle and me sharing my room, Estelle's bristly hairbrush decorating my bureau, my closet filled with her clothes, never mind all Estelle's beauty preparations in the bathroom, I got goose bumps.

"He's not so bad." I defended Walter. "Once you get to know him."

"I have no intention of ever getting to know him," Estelle said in her huffy way.

I don't think I ever exchanged a word with Walter before I went to Ms. Govoni's to sit with the kids. It's strange, but I sort of like him. I feel sorry for him. He has a sallow complexion, like Mary in *The Secret Garden*, and when he takes his glasses off, I noticed, he has lavender marks like bruises under his eyes. He said this came from wearing glasses all the time, which he has to do on account of he's blind as a bat without them. I suppose that's possible, although I've never heard that wearing glasses causes lavender marks under the eyes.

This week it was teeming rain on Saturday when Ms. Govoni came to pick me up.

"Here's the money for the paper," she said. "Although maybe Walter won't show on a day like this."

"Oh, he'll come, all right," I said. "You can count on him."

Sure enough, there he was. On the dot.

"You want me to leave this outside?" He folded his enormous black umbrella and held it out to me.

158

"For Pete's sake," I said, "don't bring it in. It'd cause a flood in here. Just leave it." He was probably the only paperboy in town who carried a large umbrella when it rained, I thought. Trust Walter. Why didn't he use a tarp to cover himself? Boys didn't use umbrellas.

"Hey." That was his usual greeting. Hey. He didn't have on a raincoat even. Or boots.

"I thought you might skip the paper today," I said. "Considering the weather."

"Neither snow nor rain nor sleet shall prevent me from prompt delivery," he said.

"That's the U.S. mail that says that," I told him. We heard scuffling in the bedroom. Rosie and Mack were getting ready for their attack.

"Let me, let me," I heard them whispering.

Mack popped out and shouted, "Brains!" and Rosie, wrapped in something that looked like an old curtain, opened her mouth to add her bit, then closed it and said, "I forgot. What was I going to say, Mack?" and the two of them went back to talk it over.

Walter bent his knees and eased himself over to the couch, preparing to sit.

"I see where they caught that guy," he said, landing, making a loud plop.

"What guy?" I said, coldness coming over me.

"The guy they've been looking for. The one they offered the reward for. Some lady over in Crawford County said she spied him hiding out in a vacant house.

159

The cops closed in. They took him off to jail, though he says he never did anything to anybody. There's a picture of him on the front page."

And expertly, like the seasoned newspaperman he was, Walter flipped open the paper. The face staring out was not a face I knew.

"That's not the one," I said, almost grinning.

"How do you know?" Walter asked in surprise.

"I just don't think that's the one," I said, blushing.

"Who knows?" Then, gazing glumly out at the streaming windows, he said, "Wanna go out?"

"Now why would anyone want to go out on a day like this?" I said.

He mumbled something, and I said, "What? I can't hear you. You're mumbling."

"I said, 'Wanna go out,' " he repeated, and when I looked at him, I tried to read his somber expression. "With me, I mean."

I laughed. It was nerves, but I did laugh. It just slipped out, the way sometimes you laugh when you don't know what else to do. I had never learned the secret of laughing at the right moment. And maybe I never would.

"You're kidding," I said. The minute I said it I was sorry. And ashamed. How tactless and rude of me. He was serious and I should've known it.

He bobbed his head at me and smiled weakly. In a flash, I recognized the hurt on his face, knew it for what it was. Lord knows I should've recognized it. I'd been there plenty of times myself. It was the look of someone who's been rejected and who knows it.

Oh, but I felt bad. How stupid can you be? I asked myself. How terrible I'd learned nothing from my considerable experience with cruelty, I thought. But not until after, after he'd gone.

"You serious?" I said, to make amends.

But he only looked at his hands and remained silent.

"Artichoke!" screamed Rosie, popping out, still in her draperies. Mack was behind her, giggling.

"Oooooh." Walter held his stomach and groaned. "Ooooooh," he said. I had to admire his courage, his timing. I couldn't have done it after a rejection like that, I knew.

"Why'd you have to go and say that word?" he demanded of Rosie and Mack. "Now if you'd gone and said 'asparagus,' well, it'd be different. But artichoke, oooooohhhh."

Rosie and Mack fell on the floor and rolled about, clutching their stomachs with great joy.

"Sure," I said when the children had taken themselves off to plan future weird words to try out on him, "I'll go out with you." Was that, I wondered, the proper way to say it? Maybe I should've said, "I'd love to go out with you," or better still, "I'll have to ask my mother."

Walter got up and opened the door, looking for his umbrella.

"Okay," he said, and sloshed off into the rain under

161

its gigantic cover. Even from the back he looked mournful.

Did he mean tomorrow, I wondered, or next month? And would we go Dutch or was he going to treat me?

I'd never been on a date before. I didn't know how to act. But then, maybe it was all new to him, too. If he was treating me, I'd pretend to have a good time. If it was Dutch, I didn't have to pretend. But I would anyway, to make up for laughing at him.

21

I have always been a dreamer. Even when I was little,
I dreamed only beautiful dreams—glorious, golden
dreams. In which only good things happened. Dressed
in something diaphanous and sparkling, like a gown Miss
America might wear, I tended, in those dreams, to sail
over treetops on invisible wings, like Peter Pan or Mary
Poppins, always coming down to earth from the sky, the
sun always shining in my eyes.

In my dreams, I arranged that the sun always shone.

And that my parents were beautiful dream parents—
accomplished, educated, rich and very loving. Parents
any child would be proud of. Just as I was the kind of
child any parent would cherish and be proud of. Together we were perfection.

And on Christmas Eve, no matter what anyone says, I dreamed I heard the reindeer and bells and somebody big and fat landing on the roof with a crash, somebody who shouted HO HO HO. Nobody can talk me out of that.

In my dreams, I always got the lead in the school play. I never forgot my lines, it goes without saying. I was the girl voted Most Likely, the girl everyone wanted, the girl who always came in first.

Once I dreamed I was in Heaven. I knew that's where I was because I was playing the harp. Someone, it may have been Saint Peter, asked what I was doing there. I said because I deserved it. I'd earned my place there. I had led a good life, I told Saint Peter, always being unselfish, always thinking of others. The expression on Saint Peter's face was a picture.

But all he did was shrug and walk away, into the whirling mist that surrounded us, and leave me alone, in all my goodness.

Now I have begun to dream of him. The dream recurs often. I look forward to it, even though as recently as this morning I woke and knew it was a foolish dream. Monday I love you. He made no sound, but I could read his lips.

I was dressed in black and playing the flute. The opera house was ablaze with light, and the audience lifted rapt faces to me, to my artistry. I was very beautiful, with my hair pulled back, showing my neat little ears, and very thin. And in the front row, he never took his eyes off me.

When my flute solo was over and the deafening applause had sunk to a mere whisper, Buster was waiting. He lifted his arms and said Please, so I took him home with me. Doris wasn't there, but Estelle was, waiting in her mother's car, which didn't have a mark on it. She said the reward was waiting for me inside. I ran to find it, but it wasn't there. There was no thousand dollars. Not that I could find. He was in the kitchen, wearing his tarp, hiding under it, and his cowboy boots. Throwing his knife up, up into the air. At some unseen target. Throwing it at me. But no matter how many times he threw it into the air, it never came back down. Yet there was always a knife in his hand.

And William and I were running, running along the boardwalk with the waves chasing us, and my hand was done up in a huge bandage that was soaked with blood.

Ah, he said, I see you are rich. Share with me. I have always wanted to be rich. Monday I love you, and I handed him the thousand dollars reward money and he kissed me and disappeared.

Forever.

When I woke, it was light outside. I could hear my mother and father in the kitchen, talking. Or was it the television?

"Well, you slept late." My mother had just done her nails. The smell of nail polish was very strong in the room. "Ms. Govoni called, said she'll be by for you early, if it's all right with you. Said she wants to take you to a lecture this afternoon, said she got a sitter for the kids." My mother waved her hand in the air to dry her nails.

"And some boy called." My mother's voice turned coy. "Said to tell you it was Walter. Said you'd know. Wouldn't give his last name. Walter?"

"It's just a boy I know," I said. It had been two Saturdays since I'd seen him. To my surprise, my mother had no comment.

"I'm going to the library," I said after I'd helped clear up the kitchen. "I have some research to do." I was planning to take out some books on child psychology. Ms. Govoni had talked to me about her studies. It sounded interesting. Maybe I'd make a good child psychologist too.

"Good girl," said my father. "More you study, more you learn." He patted me on the shoulder. "We're real proud of you, Grace. Aren't we, Grace?" he said to my mother.

"Of course," my mother said, giving her nails another coat.

On my way at last, I took the shortcut that runs down Adams Lane to the main road to the library. Adams Lane is a cul-de-sac, which is French for "dead end." I love that: "cul-de-sac." Think how much better it sounds than "dead end." Ms. Govoni says French is the most mellifluous language there is. "Mellifluous"—that means

166

"sweet sounding" or "flowing." If you know a second language, Ms. Govoni says, the world opens up to you. If you plan to travel, and I do, the knowledge of French should be very helpful.

It was one of those mornings when it was nice to be alive. I felt buoyant, a new experience—light on my feet. I felt like dancing. Maybe because, with all my exercising with Rosie and Mack, plus on my own, plus cutting out snacks and watching what I ate, I'd lost four pounds. That may not sound like much, but to me it was like losing a hundred. Even my knees felt thinner. My new bra, which was very expensive, was worth every penny. It definitely gives me a better shape. I wash it by hand every night. I'll have to buy another just like it when I save up enough money.

Think of that. Instead of saving my money to have my breasts made smaller, I'm saving my money to buy a bra, which only makes them look better, not necessarily smaller. There's a moral to that, but I'm not sure what it is.

Things were looking up. If I *did* turn out to be a child psychologist, I made up my mind I'd be a good one. I'd find some poor soul like myself, some loser who seemed destined to be an outcast for the rest of her life, and I'd turn her life around for her. With her help, of course. No one can turn another's life around without the co-operation of the person involved. You've got to work with someone, the way Ms. Govoni worked with me. It had been one lucky day in my life when she showed up.

So many things had happened, and too fast. Sometimes they blurred in my mind, like a finger painting that's been left out in the rain. Then other times, each episode stood out clearly, like a silhouette made out of black construction paper.

There's a little path at the end of Adams Lane, a footpath. Every time I walk down it, I think of the millions of feet that made that path. Probably since Colonial days feet have been treading that path. Maybe George Washington walked there. He's slept a lot of places, but no one ever took count, as far as I know, of paths he trod.

The person up ahead of me on the path was definitely not George Washington. Or even Martha. She had on shorts and an oversized sweatshirt and pink running shoes. Since I'd lost some weight, I bet I could wear shorts too. Next time I save a few bucks, maybe I'll buy some.

With a start, I realized the person ahead of me was Ashley. She was alone, a first for Ashley, who was never alone. She liked it better if she was surrounded by her minions. I'd only seen her from a distance a couple of times.

I felt myself swelling with rage and a more complicated emotion—the desire for revenge. It was now or never. This was something I had to do to regain my self-respect. If I could. If I had the nerve. This moment had been handed to me. It would never come again. If I did nothing, just walked on by, leaving Ashley intact and unscathed, it was my fault. My cowardice. I felt at that moment my whole future depended on what I did now, what I said.

I took longer steps to catch up, and I prepared my face to meet Ashley's face.

"Hello, Ashley," I said, right behind her.

She jumped, and when she saw me, her mouth tightened and she got flustered.

"I have to go back to get something," she said, taking a step backward, swerving to avoid body contact with me.

I swerved with her, boldly. I had made up my mind. She would not get away. She would not escape what I had to say. There are moments in life when your adrenaline carries you through, allows you strength you ordinarily wouldn't have. This was one of those rare moments. I'd spent the four weeks since she went for me in the girls' room planning what I'd say if I ever got the chance. There was no stopping me now.

"There's something I want to say to you," I said, quite calm.

Briefly her eyes met mine. I could see them darting wildly, swift as goldfish in a bowl. And as slippery.

"Don't bother me," Ashley said haughtily.

"You are going to listen." My voice sounded menacing and harsh, as if coming over a loudspeaker. At that moment, Ashley and I were the only two people in the world.

"Don't you touch me," she said, although I hadn't

made any move to do so. I was pleased to hear the tremble in her voice.

"You touched me," I said.

There was nothing she could say to that.

I wanted to hit her, to wound her, to cause her pain.

"Now you're going to listen to me," I told her. "It's my turn."

In a rush, I realized *I* was in control, for once. *I* was calling the shots, not Ashley. I hadn't laid a finger on her, or raised my voice, but I was in charge.

I took a deep breath and locked her slippery eyes in mine and started in.